Investigative Journalism

Everyone has seen the trope in a thousand bad sensies. I've heard it dates all the way back to old-fashioned movies and TV. Get something electrical wet, and it shorts out in spectacular fashion.

But it doesn't work in real life. Most gadgets are made of sterner stuff. Certainly, cybernetic limbs, even the ones not covered in fake skin, are waterproof. Otherwise, those who have them wouldn't be able to shower.

I stared at the prosthetic as though amazed and aghast that nothing had happened. Metal Arm barked a laugh at my idiocy, and that's when I dropped the empty glass and drove the heel of my palm into his nose.

The sucker punch snapped his head back. Presumably it flooded his eyes with blinding tears and briefly stunned him, too. But the grip of the metal hand remained as tight as before.

In a moment, he was going to come back at me hard, and even if I'd been optimistic about beating a Los Scorpiones enforcer in something approximating a fair fight, that wasn't the situation here. Other gang members were going to rush to his aid. I grabbed him as best I as was able one-handed, pivoted, and tried a clumsy hip throw.

For Erin.

Cover illustration by VIKO.

Color insert artwork by Antonio De Luca, Caroline Gariba, Nasrul Hakim,
and Lorraine Schleter.

ISBN: 978-1-63344-349-5

Printed in China.

Fantasy Flight Games
1995 West County Road B2
Roseville, MN 55113
USA

Find out more about Fantasy Flight Games
and our many exciting worlds at

www.FantasyFlightGames.com

An

Novella

Undercity

by Richard Lee Byers

Fantasy Flight Games

CHAPTER 1

"**E**veryone loves a serial killer," I said.

Jowls stubbly and grey, Sergeant Ortega had been staffing the desk at the Base de Cayambe precinct station since he fell off a slidewalk chasing a purse snatcher, broke his back, and found out the New Angeles Police Department health plan wasn't all it was cracked up to be. He glowered at me like I'd said something disgusting, instead of simply demonstrating I knew my audience.

"There's no—" Ortega paused. "Are those things on?"

"No. Look. No red light." I pointed to a spot above my right eye on the titanium-alloy frame of the vidlenses. "That means they're not recording."

Really, it didn't. I'd had the glasses modified so I could make them look like they weren't recording when they were. If somebody called my first bluff, I could even let them look through the lenses and show them displays indicating a video had been deleted when it hadn't. It helped me make a living—well, barely; until recently, anyway—documenting people who'd rather have been left alone.

"And since this is off the record," I continued, "you can be straight with me. Tell me about the serial killer."

"There isn't one."

"My sources—"

"Bums and junkies."

"—say the police have found corpses in back streets and alleys cut up Jack the Ripper–style. If that's true, the press has a right— make that a duty—to inform the people."

Ortega sneered. "Since when are you 'the press,' Zamora? The *real* press? Last time I checked, you were no better than some porno merchant shooting sensiesofts."

"Now that's just hurtful. Especially considering all the times I've slanted a piece to make the police look good. I don't have to do that, you know."

"You do if you want to stay in business and out of jail." He heaved a sigh, and some of the hostility went out of him. Maybe he was remembering the times I'd brought him his favorite takeout *hornado*—I should have thought to do it today—or maybe I just wasn't worth the energy. "Look, there's no serial killer, and I don't have time for you today. You can see we're busy." He waved his hand at the room around us.

Air-conditioned five degrees too cold, smelling of astringent cleaning products with traces of cheap perfume, blood, vomit, and unwashed and incontinent vagrant underneath, it was a harshly lit box of a place where people waited on cheap plas benches to be booked or give their statements. Streetwalkers and stim dealers. A shaken couple and two little girls: a tourist family who'd come to see the picturesque architecture of old Ecuador you can still find tucked away here and there in the district and had gotten mugged or swindled for their trouble. Androids sitting straight and quiet, here as proxies for their owners or conceivably even attending to affairs of their own, resigned to the fact that they wouldn't be seen until all the humans had been attended to.

"Yeah," I replied. "It's almost like a real police station." Not the most diplomatic thing I could have said, but that crack about not being a real journalist had gotten under my skin.

And I had a point. The precinct made a fair number of arrests, but the prisoners were all loners and bottom feeders, grifters without meaningful ties to the gangs or other powerful illegal enterprises that thrived in Base de Cayambe. The cops were reluctant to go after connected crooks no matter what crimes upright citizens reported, just like they didn't care to venture outside the "safe patrol zones." Not because they were *all* on the take but because even the honest ones doubted they could handle the blowback.

My smartass remark brought Ortega's annoyance back and ruddy blotches to his face. "Get out of here!" he said.

"I was just leaving," I said, and I did. But I only went as far as a restroom. The smell of cleaning products was stronger here, but so was the stink of puke and shit, so the odors were still playing to a tie.

Speaking of ties, I took off the fire-engine red one that everyone who knows me is used to seeing me wear every day of my life and stuck it in my pants pocket. An old flat cap—the people who know me are also used to seeing me bareheaded—came out of a jacket pocket and settled on my head, after which I took off the jacket to carry under my arm. Most importantly, I took off the vidlenses. You could buy a top-of-the-line pair that just looked like regular fashion specs, but mine were more like tinted swim goggles with tech built in, and not just because I'd saved creds when I bought them. This way, taking them off does more to change my look. Plus their very obvious nature sometimes deters those otherwise inclined to violence—who knows where I could be streaming video to at that very moment?

I'm no consummate master of disguise, but I'm pretty good at changing the way I look when I want to, and when I checked myself in the mirror, I was satisfied with the results. I just needed to change my body language to provide the finishing touches. I've been told I normally walk fast with my head hitched slightly forward, like I'm a hound on a scent. Which sounds all right to me, although I don't think the woman who was breaking up with me meant it as a compliment.

I loitered in the doorway that opens back into the reception area until Ortega got busy with another hopeful at the desk. Then I headed for the hall that holds the elevators and fell in behind half a dozen other people going the same way.

Here's a secret about the Base de Cayambe NAPD precinct building. It's a thirty-story plascrete fortress with anti-intrusion barricades. I doubt all the gangs in the district working together could blast their way in if the cops knew they were coming. But once you get inside, it's not too tricky to move around as long as you're not trying to get into the jail, the evidence lockup, or the armory. The place is just too busy and too complicated, a vast hive of offices, interrogation rooms, forensic labs, and what have you, bustling with too many cops, prosecutors, public defenders, bailiffs, technicians, and clerks for anybody to expect to recognize everybody else.

And, of course, nobody thought they needed to, because the security scanners read everybody's ID chip, but I had a programmable fake. There'd been a time when it had seemed like a smart investment. These days, maybe not so much, but since I had it, I might as well put it to use.

Anyway, I made it through a scan without an alarm going off or a trapdoor opening under my feet, and afterward I got on an elevator and traveled down to the sublevel housing the morgue. On the way, I restored my original appearance. A makeshift disguise wouldn't get me past Raul the morgue attendant. He knew me way too well. But he and I had done business in the past.

The lighting on the morgue level made the place look as stark as the reception area, but it was somehow gloomy, too, as if the dead bodies exerted their own spooky effect on the ambience. Or maybe it was just my imagination. Lounging at his own little desk, switching off whatever he was watching on his personal access device before I got a look at it, Raul seemed perfectly at ease.

"Javier Zamora," he said.

"How's it going, Raul?" I answered. "Ortega said I could go in for a minute and look around."

Raul smirked. "He did, did he? Should I call him and check?" He always felt the need to harass me a little even though we both knew exactly how this transaction would go down.

I shrugged. "Bother him if you want to. Or you could just take a break, smoke whatever, and leave me to it." I slipped a credstick out of my pocket, keyed in the proper amount for transfer to quiet Raul's imaginary scruples, and showed him the display. He nodded, and I sent him the money while regretting the necessity. You start to realize what an unfortunate, deplorable phenomenon bribery is when you can no longer afford to pay the bribes. But I hoped the investment would pay off.

"You've got fifteen minutes," he said, rising and starting down the hall. I waited until he turned a corner—so if asked, he could honestly say he hadn't seen me go into the morgue proper—then pushed through the double doors.

The morgue was even colder than it was upstairs, and here, the antiseptic smell was finally victorious—but strong enough to make your eyes sting and your head ache all by itself. If you counted the rows of drawers, you'd see the room has storage for hundreds of cadavers. Lots of people die in Base de Cayambe outside of hospitals and clinics and under suspicious or at least uncertain circumstances.

Four such unfortunates were lying on autopsy tables, but none looked like a modern-day Jack the Ripper had carved them; only the medical examiner had. I called up the room's holoscreen interface and skimmed the morgue database to find the drawers I wanted.

My viewers preferred seeing people die nasty deaths, sudden and brutal or protracted and painful. When I couldn't give them that, they liked close-up inspections of the corpses where they dropped, maybe in the gutter and gnawed by rats to make the spectacle that much more sordid. But naked bodies laid out in identical fashion in the clinical sterility of a morgue are degraded and dehumanized in their own special way, and I'd found that, properly hyped and presented, they satisfied the fans well enough.

Certainly, these corpses wouldn't disappoint. I was years past the point when I'd still flinched at things other than the prospect of imminent pain to myself, but as I slid the drawers rumbling open one by one, I came closer than I had in a while.

The face of the first victim, thus far unidentified like the others, had mostly been cut away along with portions of the bone and brain behind it, leaving a cavity you could stick your fist in if you were so inclined. The autopsy report said the pieces hadn't been found and speculated the killer had carried them away as trophies. The liver and kidneys were gone as well.

The second body was like a sagging, half-empty, tattered sack. Except for the spinal column, the killer had pulled most of the bones below the sternum out of the body. Most of the organs from the lower torso, too.

The mutilations to the last were in a sense more superficial but equally hard to look at. Though leaving a bruised and battered square-jawed face intact, the killer had flayed the greater part of the skin from the raw muscle beneath and taken the genitals as well. Who knew, maybe for dessert.

The damage was so gruesome it was difficult to see past it, but it might make for a better story if I didn't just pass on the ME's observation that the victims were "unidentified" and let it go at that. I gave each of them a second look.

Though given their current condition, it was difficult to be sure, my guess was that they'd all had reasonably well-developed, well-defined musculature. There wasn't much in the way of scars or calluses on their hands and feet. The nails were well cared for. The first body had a tattoo of a butterfly on the chest that beat its bright blue wings and flew around, and the second had ripples of iridescence running through long brunette hair, tingeing it red, then purple, then green. Without body heat to power them, the skin art moved sluggishly and the flowing highlights in the hair had faded. They were dying like their owners, just more slowly.

Behind me, a lightly accented alto voice said, "What the hell!" Startled, I jerked around.

Detective Helen Bradley was ash-blond, grey-eyed, and pale; a Londoner originally, she was one of the millions who had immigrated to New Angeles to make it the biggest as well as the most important megapolis in the world. Sometimes she and I got along. Judging from the way she was glaring at me, this wasn't going to be one of those times.

"Where's Raul?" she asked.

I shrugged. "Nobody at the desk when I got here. I let myself in."

"Of course you did. Did you snap vid of the bodies?"

"I'd never do that without permission." I pointed to indicate the little red light on the glasses was still off.

"Of course you wouldn't." She strode to the first victim's drawer and shoved it shut with a clank.

"You're losing the ability to trust, Detective. It's sad. But I'm still glad to see you. How about answering some questions?"

"About this? Not a chance." She shoved the body with the missing bones back inside the wall.

"If there's a serial killer running wild in Base de Cayambe, I have a right to report it, and the public has a right to know."

She made a spitting sound. "Has that line ever worked on anyone?"

"Not yet, but after I try it ten times, I get a free *gyrrito*. Do the police have any leads?"

She slammed the third victim's drawer. "No comment."

"Any theory on why each of the victims was mutilated in a very different fashion from the others?"

"No comment."

"These are just the most recent victims. Are there previous ones who've already been processed through the morgue? Tell me about those."

"What part of 'no comment' do you not understand?"

"Jesus Christ, Bradley, if this went public, it could help you catch the guy. People would come to you with tips."

"False leads, and we'd have to waste time investigating every one of them."

"Investigating anything might make a nice change of pace for you."

Bradley scowled. "Tourists come to the district looking for authentic traditional Ecuadoran this and that. Travelers going up or just down from the Beanstalk spend money in restaurants, bars, and hotels. Get everybody panicked over a serial killer, and all that goes away, and for what? People get murdered all over the district all the time anyway. If there is a serial killer—and I'm not confirming there is—their crimes are just one more drop in a big, overflowing bucket of blood. Now get out of here; find some other dirt to feed to the vultures who watch your stuff, or I'll charge you with trespassing in a restricted area and interfering with an ongoing investigation."

"None of that would stick," I said, and it might have come across as more dauntless and defiant if I hadn't followed it up with, "but I'm going." I sensed I'd pushed her as far as I could.

As I stepped out of the precinct building, my body straightened at the possibility of sunlight. Base de Cayambe rises—and descends—layer upon layer. The tallest structure visible is the Beanstalk, the space elevator, the bright future of humanity if you believe the Weyland Consortium's PR. Dwarfed by it but still looming over puny little human beings are starscrapers and arcologies connected by elevated slidewalks and mag-lev tracks, while below these are levels of factories, warehouses, tenements, assorted dens of vice, and ultimately cave-like spaces frequented only by the destitute and desperate. Everything casts its shadow on what's beneath it, and the lower you go, the more you find yourself in places that are roofed over or enclosed entirely. As a result, sunshine is a rare pleasure for all but a relative few. Still, the police had placed their headquarters high enough on a hill and far enough away from even taller buildings that it wasn't unreasonable to hope I might catch a little.

I didn't, though. It was the wrong time of day, and the sun was in the wrong position. Even after getting away from the precinct house, I was in the shadow of the Beanstalk, which swept slowly across the city as if the space elevator were a colossal sundial. Or as if to drive home the point that rejects like myself had no claim on sunlight anymore. Shoulders slumping, in my head, I told humanity's gateway to the solar system to go screw itself.

As I tramped away heading gradually downward, past spacers, students, Bohemian types who managed to be gaudy and shabby at the same time, and blue, metal bioroids putting up a building while a couple of morose humans picketed the job site, I tried to figure out what to do with what I'd learned so far. It was more difficult than I'd expected.

The easy and arguably smart and safe thing to do was to run with what I had: the video of the corpses, what I'd gleaned from the coroner's notes, and Bradley's stonewalling. It might be enough for one of the Network infotainment channels I had a relationship with to pick the story up, and if not, I had my own little personal outlet with a few subscribers eager to see everything weird and lurid the undercity had to offer—only vicariously, without risking their own precious necks or reputations. One way or another, I'd make a few credits, and I wasn't all that worried about the police.

True, I didn't fully understand Bradley's attitude: threats from a cop are rarely any fun, and I did need a level of tolerance from the police to stay in business. But they knew me and more or less accepted that, like everyone else in the district, I was out for myself and did what I had to do to make ends meet. If I reported what I had, I'd be wise to avoid them for a while, but eventually somebody else's fresher offense would eclipse the memory of mine, I'd have the chance to do a cop a favor, and my relationship with the precinct would reset to what it had been—provided I hadn't annoyed them any further in the meantime.

Yeah, that was the intelligent way to go, but it wasn't the only way, and as I wandered by a fenced-off building site, the other option tugged at me despite myself. A seccam turned on its mount to track me in my folly, and a flying surveillance drone buzzed overhead.

There was too much about the murders I didn't understand; some of the details I hadn't even had a chance to ask Bradley about before she sent me on my way. The things I couldn't explain ticked my investigative reporter's instincts, rusty though they were. They teased me with the possibility that, explored fully, this could be a *big* story and considerably more lucrative. Conceivably, it might even land me back in a job where a lousy ray of sunlight didn't thrill me and missing out on one didn't depress me. A long shot, but stranger things had happened.

And the truth was, I *needed* it to be considerably more lucrative. My channel had kept me afloat for a while, but these days, I was losing viewers. Why, I didn't know. Just the fickleness of the public, maybe, but whatever the reason, I was sinking deeper and deeper into debt. If I didn't want to end up another starving bum on the streets of the undercity, only a big score would turn things around.

Besides, somewhat to my surprise, the story intrigued me for its own sake. It made me want to use skills I'd barely exercised in a while. I still called myself a journalist, and bristled when anyone suggested I wasn't, but the truth was, it didn't take a Pulitzer Prize winner to find bizarre, salacious, and squalid scenes for my audience to shake their disapproving heads over, drool over, or react to some other way. In Base de Cayambe, such sights were all around me. I just had to point my vidlenses and eyes in the right direction and blink the REC command.

By the time I passed Sensie Palace with its holodisplay trailers playing over and over again on the sidewalk, their characters oblivious to impatient pedestrians marching right through them, I'd decided to hold off posting the story while I kept poking around. Surely the cops wouldn't be *that* angry about it, and I didn't see any other downside.

Worn stone steps littered with used condoms, discarded Happy Patches, and broken bottles—we locals really do cherish the neighborhood's quaint, archaic beauty—took me down to a gloomy spot where the last tiny slivers of sky had disappeared and all the light was artificial, much of it neon, blazing to lure customers to raucous strip joints and little bodegas selling off-brand wine, candy, and T-shirts. I was back home in the undercity, but for once, it was all right. It was where I needed to be to continue my investigation.

CHAPTER 2

If you've heard of Base de Cayambe's undercity at all, you may well have heard of Evil Eye. Located on the main drag of Mercado Baja, the district's teeming marketplace for unlicensed vendors and outright contraband, it caters to wylders, off-gridders, and similar exotic types, while a flashing neon sign reading "Freaks Only" warns off everybody else. As I approached, the music pounding inside was already audible, and three spacers, identifiable by their smart coveralls and the careful way they moved in Earth gravity, went in ahead of me. When the door opened, strobing light flashed out.

I sauntered up to the two bouncers bracketing the entrance. Bare to the waist, they were all muscle, bristly hair, leathery hide, tusks, and snout. If they turned around, you saw they even had holes cut in the seats of their formfitting shorts to accommodate curly little tails.

A wylder can pay gene-tailors and cosmetic surgeons to give them the superficial features of pretty much any animal. Add a magnificent rack of antlers here, a gorgeous mottling of spotted fur there. Even, for the wylder with money to burn, feathers in place of hair—atop the head or on limbs, like wings. Emilio and Vicente had chosen to look like hogs. There's no accounting for taste.

When the bouncers saw me coming, and the dot of red light glowing on my glasses, they struck flexing bodybuilder poses that showed off their physiques to best advantage. While a lot of people in the undercity prefer to go unrecorded, Emilio and Vicente aren't criminals—mostly—and you probably don't become a wylder if you don't want people looking at you.

"Hi, guys," I said. "How's it going?"

"Fine," Emilio said, "except that this one still wants to get the trotters." Thanks to the tusks, his voice was a little hard to understand, a price he paid to be the chimera he wanted to be.

"Why stop short of perfection?" Vicente oinked in reply.

"Because we already owe too much, and it will take you weeks to learn to stand and walk again, weeks when I'll have to pull double shifts because you aren't able to work." Emilio sighed and looked back at me, perhaps for support. "It's hard being the practical one."

"Sometimes," I said, trying to sound like I wasn't taking sides. "I'm hoping the two of you can help me with something."

"What's that?" Vicente asked.

I took out my PAD and showed them still images of the faces of the second and third victims. Since the first corpse no longer had a face, there wasn't much point in displaying that shot. "Recognize them?"

"No," Emilio said. "Should we?"

"You heard about the serial killer?" I asked.

"No," Vicente said. "Is there one?"

"If there is, these are two of the victims. Unidentified so far, but I don't think they lived here in the undercity. They had the kind of physiques you get when you go to a health club and maybe even have a personal trainer and nutritionist nagging you to take better care of yourself." I remembered what that was like. "One of them had one of those expensive rainbow hair rinses, and another victim had fancy animated skin art. A custom job, I'm almost sure. My theory is that the murderer targets well-to-do area residents who come down here slumming or tourists from out of town. If I can find somebody who remembers seeing one of them, maybe that will give me a line on when and where the vic crossed paths with the killer."

Emilio fingered one of his tusks as he pondered what I'd said. "If you're right, wouldn't somebody be making a stink about solid citizens disappearing? Wouldn't the cops have told everybody they're looking for a serial killer?"

I shrugged. "The theory's a work in progress. You're sure you haven't seen either of these people? You didn't have to turn them away when they tried to get into the club?"

"Not that I remember," Vicente said. "Do you want to ask around inside?" I never knew whether to be flattered or offended that, normal though I looked, he and his partner considered me a "freak" in good standing.

I transferred a tip from my credstick to the bouncers' joint account—another bet I was placing on the story paying off and couldn't really afford to lose—and made my way into dazzling, deafening chaos where the drunk and the high jostled one another on a packed dance floor, rope dancers with phosphorescent skin whirled above them, and the glow of the cocktails flashed in time to the music.

Asking questions in that environment was about as easy and successful as you'd expect. After I got hoarse shouting—and a drunken off-gridder who didn't appreciate being interrupted while he was trying to talk price with a pencil-thin hooker with scales, fangs, and a forked tongue threatened to beat me up—I decided to try my luck someplace else.

The question was where. Thinking the victims might have come to the undercity to shop for bargains or for merchandise they didn't care to buy through legal, traceable channels, I'd already canvassed many of the stalls and shops in the Low Market. I'd also gone to the Ani-ink tattoo parlor, the Cavern Tavern, the Hothouse, New Heads for Old, and many of the other bars, brothels, stim-flops, narcodispensaries, casinos, and assorted dens of vice an outsider might have heard of and wanted to visit, conceivably because they'd seen the joint showcased in one of my own reports. Now that I'd come up empty in all of them, what did that leave?

Well, one place. The trick would be getting in. Unlike Evil Eye and other shady establishments where I'm welcome or at least tolerated, Hoyo Rojo had banned me, and even if they hadn't made a special point of that, no one is admitted without a membership card or invitation.

I bought a plas lighter and a pack of cigarillos in a hole-in-the-wall shop, then retired to the restroom. There, I went to work altering my appearance. The vidlenses and red tie came off. I combed stain into my hair to make it look like I was going grey. Back on the street, I smoked three of the skinny brown unfiltered cigars in quick succession, getting used to them once more and getting the smell of the smoke on my breath and body. Normally, I don't smoke, so if you see someone chain-smoking, it can't be me, can it?

Then I walked the two blocks from the market proper, past glowing gang tags on accordion shutters and grey walls. To those who could read them in all their subtlety, they proclaimed that this or that dark, seemingly locked-up building was actually open for business to the passerby who craved a kinky night with an android, Sting to amp up their adrenal response and switch off their pain receptors while they settled a score in a fistfight, or a Skorpios-made fletcher pistol or HHI-model combat shotgun for an even more definitive resolution to a dispute.

Periodically, street-level stim dealers called out offering their wares. Once, someone tried to sneak up behind me. Despite their attempt at stealth, their rubber-soled shoes squeaked on the pavement. The thought flashing through my head that maybe *I* had become the serial killer's next target, I pivoted, glowered, and stuck my hand in my coat pocket as though I had a weapon. The scrawny teenager who'd been creeping up on me bolted, and I decided he'd been just another would-be mugger after all.

Ironically, the block containing Hoyo Rojo looked marginally more respectable than the one leading up to it. Relatively innocuous storefronts were open in a straightforward way, offering what their neon and holodisplays proclaimed. For the moment, I ignored the payday loan business in favor of an old-fashioned hashish bar. It'll sell you a drink, too, but the main attraction is the water pipes on all the tables and the varieties of hash available to fill them. Sitting in the hazy, aromatic atmosphere, you can fire one up and get high the way our ancestors did back in the last millennium.

On the whole, Base de Cayambe prefers faster, stronger, and edgier highs—like stim and its cousins—so the place wasn't busy. But two nicely dressed young men—*they* looked like serial-killer bait—were knocking back shots of *aguardiente* and sucking on the mouthpieces of their hookah, holding in the smoke as long as they could and then coughing it out. Neither looked like he was enjoying himself very much. They looked like they were trying to dull the memory of something they'd just experienced, and that made perfect sense considering that one had a red plas card peeking out of the breast pocket of his blazer.

I'm no Sherlock Holmes, but once in a while you can size people up and make a pretty good guess about what's going on with them. My hunch was that the young men had been part of a group a member had brought to Hoyo Rojo and, unable to stomach what they'd seen, had fled across the street. They hadn't gone any farther because they were waiting for the rest of their party to reappear.

I ordered a Sol Dorado at the bar and waited for the guy with the card to stand up and head for the restroom. I did the same and contrived to bump into him at the start of the little hallway. In that moment, I plucked the red plas rectangle from his pocket and slipped it into my own.

I'm no master pickpocket, either, but I learned the basics years ago when I did a series on the thieves and con artists of the undercity, and impaired people make the easiest marks. My victim didn't notice the lift, and I figured that if he realized the card was missing later, he wouldn't care anyway. Why should he when he didn't *want* to get back into Hoyo Rojo?

I crossed the street to the payday loan operation, a seedy little storefront that really only exists to serve as a security checkpoint on the way into "the Hole." The sole employee was a wylder with the fangs and black fur of a gorilla. Unless his apelike physique was wholly artificial, he hadn't truly needed the surgeon to establish a resemblance. His frame made Emilio and Vicente look puny.

His real job was to make people who didn't belong feel unwelcome, turn around, and leave, and given that I'd been expressly told to stay away, his glare certainly intimidated me. Trying to look as if it hadn't, I casually waved the red card for his inspection—or, more accurately, for inspection by the sensor that read the chip inside.

The gatekeeper stared at me for another second or two, more than enough time for me to think *Shit, he saw through my disguise, or something's wrong with the card.* Then he grunted—it sounded convincingly gorilla-ish—and concealed doors in the back wall opened. I gave him a nod and descended the red-painted carbo-concrete steps on the other side.

The stairs ended on the bottom level of the club, which meant I was on the same level as the combatants in the fighting pit but separated from them by chain-link fence. Here, there was nowhere to sit, and unless a person managed to push right up to the fence, it was actually easier to see from the arena-style seats and balconies higher up, especially with holoscreens offering close-up views of the action. Even so, the lowest level was packed with people who felt a visceral need to be as near as possible to the violence, near enough to hear bone crack and metal crash and to smell the sweat, blood, and oil.

On every level, gleaming bioroid cashiers sold tickets and paid off winners behind old-fashioned betting windows. The trans-actions could have been handled via PADs or credsticks and the Network, and essentially, they were. But apparently management thought the cashiers and such contributed to the atmosphere and encouraged heavier wagering.

Above the windows, betting boards told the punters what they could wager on and what the odds were, numbers that flickered and changed from moment to moment. The bets, however, weren't on which fighter would win. Everybody knew that going in.

The match currently underway was a case in point. A big woman semidressed in leather belts and bands was chasing a screaming, pleading clone—a black-haired Chikao-model—around the fight-ing pit with a kind of short-range flamethrower. The android had a transplas shield to block the bursts of flame but no offensive weapon of his own, not that he would have been capable of using it on a human being anyway. Thus, the betting was on how long he'd last, exactly what sort of injury would take him down, and whether or not he'd survive it for any length of time.

Such fights are the reason I'm persona non grata. Back when I was establishing my second career—exploring the undercity, figur-ing out what I could get away with and what I couldn't—I'd per-suaded a member to take me into Hoyo Rojo. Though by then I'd seen other fight clubs, the naked, gloating sadism of this one dis-gusted me. When I put my feature up on the Net, I made the stupid mistake of acting like I was still a reporter for NBN with the might of the company supposedly protecting me. I gave in to the temptation to editorialize and, worse, to refrain from blurring the faces of spectators who'd been in the crowd. Shortly thereafter, toughs cornered me in an alley, beat me up, and warned me never to come back.

As I took my first look around, I couldn't help feeling that might well have been good advice. Ignoring that sensible judgment, and recognizing that it would be impossible to talk to anyone amid the screaming frenzy at pit level, I climbed a different set of stairs to a platform where drinks and other concessions were available. By the time I got there, the match was ending. The human faked low, the clone dipped the shield to protect his legs, and she straightened up fast and blasted yellow fire in his face. His hair caught, and he burned to death in under a minute, tingeing the air with the smell of burned meat. Winning bettors cheered and headed for the windows while losers tore up their tickets and dropped the pieces on the floor.

Telling myself I didn't care or, if I couldn't help caring a little, not to let it show, I bought another Sol Dorado and started chatting up my fellow spectators. When I felt I'd established sufficient rapport, I showed the person I was talking to the faces of Victims Two and Three and asked if they recognized them.

While I was busy with that and getting nowhere, down in the pit, emaciated half-naked guys with stringy, matted hair—homeless people, by the looks of them—attacked a bioroid with the spiky medieval-style maces they'd been given. Each of the humans had multiple Happy Patches plastered on him, and they stumbled and looked as if, from moment to moment, they were having trouble remembering where they were and what they were supposed to be doing. The bioroid's arms ended in whirring chainsaws instead of hands, but it was as incapable as the Chikao clone had been of using them to hurt humans. The match was intended to be funny, and the spectators howled with laughter. I pushed away the thought that the audience I'd cultivated might well have reacted the same.

Eventually one of the drugged men tripped and stumbled onto the blade of a chainsaw despite the bioroid's frantic effort to snatch it out of the way. Blood sprayed, the fans cheered and guffawed, and at that instant, I spotted two burly men striding across the concession area. They were coming straight at me.

I couldn't say how I'd been made. It was possible human eyes or some facial recognition program had penetrated my disguise, or maybe somebody thought my asking questions was odd enough that it should be reported. Either way, it was clearly in my best interest to get the hell out of there.

Spitting out my latest cigarillo, I took a fast glance around. Like any such establishment, Hoyo Rojo has doors opening to service areas intended only for staff, but for one reason or another, none looked particularly accessible, nor could I be sure they'd be unlocked if I did get to them. I decided my best option was the sole public entrance, the one I'd come through on the bottom level, even though, in this case, *best* was hardly the same thing as *good*.

I started walking toward the stairs. I had it in my head that if I didn't run, the guys chasing me wouldn't either for fear of alarming the crowd, but I was wrong. When I moved, they dashed, and I had to do the same and shove people aside to stay ahead of them.

Once I reached the top of the stairs, I saw that two more toughs were climbing up to intercept me. I ran straight at them, playing chicken, hoping they might flinch at the prospect of me barreling into them at full speed and knocking them backward down the steps. I was wrong again. They kept coming.

I dodged into one of the less densely packed rows of stadium seating. I still stepped on and tripped over people's feet, jostled them, and elicited snarls and curses, but it was possible to stumble my way down the row.

After several seconds, I came to a spot where the seat in front of me was empty, and, descending below me, I could make out a zigzag route of similarly unoccupied places. Bounding from one to the next, *maybe* I could make it to the bottom without tumbling headlong and breaking my neck.

As I attempted to do just that, I kept glancing to the side to see what my pursuers were up to. A couple had stayed on the stairs and were pacing me, waiting to catch me if I doubled back. The other two had chased me into the tiers of benches. Fortunately, the spectators were getting in their way just as they'd gotten in mine, and neither was on the brink of grabbing me just yet.

The show the Happy-Patched vagrants and the bioroid were putting on was entertaining enough that a fair number of people hadn't noticed the chase was happening. But some had. An off-gridder with a dozen facial piercings, each bar and ring blinking with LEDs, and a merman wylder with a crest running over the top of his hairless green head and pink gill slits opening and closing on the sides of his neck jumped up and turned around to catch me—motivated, perhaps, by the same bully's mentality that made them enjoy watching hopelessly overmatched "fighters" get mauled in the pit.

I try to avoid fights. In Base de Cayambe, the desire to prove how tough you are is all too likely to get you killed. But there are also times when only fighting will save your life, and after landing in the undercity, I'd had to learn something about self-defense. I hoped my mediocre skills were good enough to get me past the two creeps blocking the way.

Piercings pulled back his arm for a roundhouse punch when I bounded into range. Striking first, I rammed the heel of my hand into his nose, breaking it. He lurched back, lost his balance, and toppled over onto people in the row below him.

So far, so good, but when I pivoted, Fishguy was lunging, arms spread, coming in low for a tackle. Out of time to react, teetering off-balance on the tier of seating above his, I had no doubt he was going to succeed in wrapping his arms around my legs.

As he did, I pitched forward, flopping on top of him, and slammed elbow strikes into his back. After the third one, he grunted, and his grip on my lower legs loosened. I kicked free, scrambled down the length of him, clambered to my feet, and ran on.

My next problem was that the stadium seating didn't go all the way to pit level. The shelf containing the first row ended in an overhang above the spectators on the floor. As I swung myself over the low guardrail at the end, I winced to see that a fall of about fifteen feet awaited me and that there was nowhere to land but on top of the mob below. Still, with the Hole's security goons closing in, my only chance was to jump.

I could easily have ended up jamming some vulnerable part of me into somebody's hard head and incapacitating or even killing myself, but I didn't. Bodies folded beneath me, cushioning my fall, and I had the wind knocked out of me but suffered nothing worse. Hoping I hadn't done irreparable damage to any of the squirming people under me, either, I floundered on their backs, jumped up, and scurried on. I had to twist and push my way through the press, but it wasn't as bad as it could have been. I guess I now seemed erratic enough that people made an effort to clear me a path.

Grinning, I threw open the door to the red stairs and escape. The wylder with the gorilla g-mods was right on the other side. An alarm or call had summoned him down from the payday loan office to help catch me.

He swung one furry elongated arm in a backhand blow, and his fist clipped me on the jaw and rocked me backward. I tried to shake off the shock and recover my balance, but before I could, he grabbed me, threw me down on the floor, crouched on top of me. I struggled in vain to push the gorilla off, but he pounded my head against the carboconcrete floor until I passed out.

I woke when I reflexively twisted my nose away from the ammonia sting of smelling salts. That sent a stab of pain through my head that grudgingly subsided into a steady throbbing. Trying to move as little and as carefully as possible thereafter, I surveyed my surroundings as best I could. My vision was blurry, and at certain moments, I saw two of everything.

I'd been hauled into a bustling space that amounted to the Hoyo Rojo locker room, infirmary, repair shop, and recycling center. A Tenma-line clone with a shock of white hair stood in the middle of the floor next to a drain. Tenmas are designed to drive and pilot vehicles, and this one was even dressed in a chauffeur's uniform, but the twitching eyes and clenching and unclenching fists suggested he'd been repurposed to fight either via sophisticated reconditioning or good old-fashioned abuse. Bashed and broken into nonfunction, the bioroid with chainsaws for hands slouched in a corner with viscous, bluish fluid leaking out of it.

As for me, I was strapped into a kind of bulky motorized wheelchair. I had a ball and chain locked around my left ankle, too, like a convict in an old cartoon. At the moment, the latter was completely unnecessary, but it wouldn't be if my captors wheeled *me* into the pit and let me out of the seat. They'd have to do that for me to put on any kind of a show before my opponent took me apart as they surely would. When all the fights on the card were mismatches, it wasn't tough to guess which role the guy with the concussion and the leg iron was supposed to play.

A stooped, grey-haired woman, another Hoyo Rojo employee, had administered the smelling salts. When she stepped away, I saw the gorilla wylder slouching behind her with knuckles on the floor. The ape bared his teeth at me and flicked a telescoping carbosteel combat baton out to full extension. Apparently he doubled as a fighter, and I was his victim for tonight.

A pang of fear stabbed through me, but perhaps I still had a chance. Standing with the wylder was Mr. Chen, short, plump, dressed in an expensive suit and tie that reflected what was around him like mirrors, and smiling his customary close-lipped, meaningless half smile. I don't know who owns Hoyo Rojo, but Chen manages it, and his presence suggested that *maybe* I could talk my way out of this situation.

I composed myself as best I could—never look scared unless you can see a tactical advantage to it—and said, "Good evening, Mr. Chen."

He gave me a nod in return. The small motion split him into two figures for a moment. "Mr. Zamora," he replied.

"How did you spot me?" I asked. I didn't much care, but anything to get him chatting. I hoped it would give me time to think of compelling arguments for releasing me unharmed. Failing that, it might at least delay the punishment in store.

"Our Ms. Aquino saw through your disguise," he said. "I gather she watches your videos."

"Always nice to hear from a fan." Outside the locker room, the crowd bellowed, probably because someone had just landed a telling attack. If so, the current match would be over soon.

"I was under the impression you learned your lesson after your previous visit," said Chen. "I never imagined you'd seek to do a follow-up report."

"Someone should," I said. "I saw the drugged man stumble onto the chainsaw. That was over the line."

Chen waved away my squeamishness and so conjured another moment of double vision. "He signed the waiver, and in any case, no one dies here who will be missed."

"Look," I said, "the point is, I *didn't* come back to do another story on Hoyo Rojo. Nobody saw me wearing my vidlenses, did they?"

"It would have been a poor disguise indeed if you had." Beyond the door that led to the arena, the spectators roared again, even louder this time.

"I was asking questions about something that really has nothing to do with the club," I said. "Check with the people I talked to."

"That's unnecessary," he said. "Your purpose for coming is irrelevant. What matters is that you disobeyed the instruction to stay away."

The crowd outside the door shouted, the largest outcry yet. Instinct or perhaps just fear told me the match had ended. Now the winner would exit the pit, and the loser would almost certainly be carried out. Someone might tidy up the space a little, and the spectators would be given time to place their bets on the next fight. Then the simian wylder and I would be locked inside the chain-link fence.

"What if I was working to catch a serial killer?" I asked.

Chen shrugged. "I haven't heard of such, and even if I had, it would have nothing to do with me."

"It would cut into your profits," I said, "if people were scared to come to the undercity and your club."

"Then it will be just as well if you're in no condition to report the story." Possibly operating on some sort of timer, his suit and tie stopped being mirrors and became vidscreens where three men in old-fashioned sailor suits danced in black and white.

The bursts of sound from outside the room had jolted me. The quiet was gnawing at me. How much time had passed since the end of the previous fight, and how long was the break between matches?

"People know I'm here," I said, wishing it were so.

Chen turned up his soft pink hands. "Who's to say you actually arrived? Even if you did…I don't mean to offend you, Mr. Zamora, but as I explained, no one comes to harm in the pit whom anyone would miss."

I struggled to think of something else, anything else, I could say to persuade him. Sweat ran down from my hairline. My mouth was dry, my throat clogged.

A pimply teenager in a stretched-out Human First T-shirt way too big for him—handed down, bought secondhand, or scavenged, I supposed—stuck his head in the door. "Pit's ready," he said. Already excited, the gorilla wylder perked up even more.

"Please," I said, "don't do this. You're setting yourself up for trouble you don't need."

"Isn't that the very essence of life?" Chen answered. "Chair, go to the pit." The wheelchair rolled forward.

I was sure that once it carried me through the door, there would be no avoiding a beating that would lay me up for weeks, possibly maim me for life, or maybe even kill me. I doubted Chen meant to walk along with me and continue our conversation, and even if he did, once the crowd saw me heading for the pit, they'd be sorely disappointed if I got a last-minute reprieve. No impresario would want that.

"Did my story *really* hurt the club?" I asked. The wheelchair carried me past Chen, and even though it hurt, I twisted my head to maintain eye contact for another moment. "I bet it didn't. I bet *more* customers started showing up."

Chen hesitated for just a tick. Then he said, "Perhaps. Still, you showed the faces of people who expected anonymity, and you came back when you were warned not to."

By the time he finished speaking, I couldn't see him at all anymore no matter how hard I strained, and the wheelchair was most of the way to the exit. The gorilla wylder leered, pulled the door open, and said, "After you."

"I'll do *another* feature on Hoyo Rojo!" I babbled. "I'll play up how hardcore and sick the place is, but this time, without embarrassing any of your customers! I'll work mentions of the club into other stories! It will be like an ad campaign! You'll pack people in!"

My seat reached the threshold. Then Chen said, "Chair, stop," and it did. He told it "Turn around and bring the passenger back to me." After an instant spent processing the new command, it did that, too.

"You understand," said Chen, "that if you fail to keep your word, I'll have to address that, too."

"Sure," I said, and then suspicion belatedly popped into my head. "Were you really going to put me in the pit, or did you just want to see how badly you could scare me?"

"Consider poor Rodrigo." I assumed Chen meant my intended opponent. "Doesn't he look genuinely disappointed?"

Maybe he did at that. The gorilla face made it a little hard to tell. At any rate, I decided the only thing that truly mattered was that, for whatever reason, I'd been spared.

"How about letting me out of the chair?" I said.

"Chair, release the passenger," said Chen. My restraints unfastened themselves and retracted. "Leg iron, unlock yourself." The metal cuff around my ankle hummed and clicked open.

The first time I tried to stand, weakness and dizziness dumped me back down onto the seat. From a purely physical standpoint, it would have been easier just to stay there, but I couldn't bear to remain in a position where Chen could lock me down again with just a word. I took a couple deep breaths, gripped the armrests, and managed to rise, after which I stepped behind the chair and gripped the back to hold myself up.

"You needn't start preparing your new story this very night," said Chen. "You can return when you're feeling more yourself. Rodrigo will have a pass waiting for you at the desk upstairs." He turned away.

"Wait," I said.

He turned back and raised an eyebrow. "Yes?"

"I came here to ask questions. Mind if I ask them of you?"

"About your serial killer."

"Yes."

"Mr. Zamora, I have many important matters requiring my attention…but I admit to being ever so slightly intrigued. Very well. I'll give you another minute. Tell me about the murders."

I did, and when I finished, I showed him the pictures I'd stored on my PAD. He didn't recognize the second victim, but he studied the third for several seconds and then said, "Interesting."

I felt a surge of excitement. "They came here?"

"Yes, but not to sit in the audience. He wanted to go into the cage. We established he had no training or background as a fighter, and I explained that if he did go in, it would be as the underdog. That didn't deter him. I had the sense he'd be entertaining, and so I acceded to his request. I suppose he could have received the bruises in the picture during the course of the murder, but they could also be souvenirs from what he experienced here. I remember he was quite battered and bloodied when he left."

"He was a masochist, then." In the undercity, someone like that could find plenty of people willing to beat them up for a fee or just for fun, but maybe for Victim Three, the humiliation of being knocked around in front of scores of people added to the thrill.

Chen shook his head. "I don't think so. He wanted the compensation. I'd even say he was desperate for it, desperate like the derelicts and addicts who land here, desperate enough to suffer harm to obtain it."

"That doesn't make sense."

Chen shrugged. The dancing sailors vanished, and his suit and tie turned a luminous green.

"Did he tell you his name?"

"No, and now I really must leave you. Rodrigo will show you out."

By the time I stumbled toward the arena exit, the gorilla wylder escorting me but making no effort to steady me, the next match was underway, and most of the spectators were too busy watching three Brazilian mastiffs attack a Henry clone trying to fend them off with a bullwhip to pay any attention to me.

Up in the stadium seating, though, one guy turned to watch me go by. He was tall and lanky, and his right arm was prosthetic. I could tell because it didn't have flesh-colored plastic covering the silvery metal and he'd chopped off the sleeves of his black leather motorcycle jacket and the shirt beneath to put it on display. The limb had copper-colored, scorpion-shaped studs on it that matched the tattoo on his neck.

As if I hadn't already been through enough that night, I felt a fresh twinge of trepidation. Los Scorpiones aren't the biggest criminal organization in all New Angeles, but here in Base de Cayambe, their home turf, they're as powerful as any and tend to specialize in the more violent forms of illegal activity. People generally hope to avoid their attention.

But I'd reported on them before without provoking any sort of reprisal. I had the sense that some of them had even enjoyed the notoriety. I couldn't think of any reason for one of them to stare down at me now except simple curiosity at my battered look and limping progress. Surely it was only leftover shakiness from the pain and fear I'd experienced previously that made me worry it might be something more.

CHAPTER 3

The quality of medical care in Base de Cayambe varies greatly depending on where you go and how much you have to spend. Fortunately, even the hole-in-the-wall walk-in clinic down the street from Hoyo Rojo could handle a simple concussion and some bruises.

Unfortunately, my finances couldn't really handle the bill. But I couldn't see much of a choice, and so the story that was supposed to put credits into my account kept right on sucking them out.

After my no-frills, what's-a-bedside-manner treatment, four pain pills, and several hours of deep, sedated sleep, I was more or less my old self again. That was good, because the following day involved a lot of walking and even more frustration.

I hadn't come close to identifying Victim Three yet, but once I thought about it, I decided I knew something about him I didn't know about the others. Until recently, he'd been a prosperous sort—recently enough that he still had the gym muscles, expensive haircut, and what have you—but then he'd fallen on hard times. That was why he'd been willing to take a public beating for money.

It also suggested he'd been living here in the seedy part of Base de Cayambe with the rest of us *plebeyos*, not just visiting. Thus, I began working my way from one flophouse to the next asking the supers and anyone else I ran into if he'd been a tenant.

The problem was that New Angeles is the biggest city that ever existed, every district is huge, and as the conduit for traffic to and from the Beanstalk, Base de Cayambe offers even more cheap housing and transient accommodations than the rest of them. As the hours passed, and I grew weary and footsore, I started to think I could do this for weeks without finding the right place. But when you only have one thin potential lead, you just keep chasing it.

Night was falling as I trudged up to yet another tenement. I knew it was falling because automated systems were switching on more exterior lights even though this deep in Base de Cayambe, shrouded in the shadows of the colossal buildings looming above, it had essentially been dark all day anyway. A guy wearing an old military uniform was nodding in a rocker on the porch. The patches indicated he'd seen combat on Luna and Mars both, but he didn't look like anyone's idea of a war hero anymore. Something—maybe the lingering effects of radiation or a bioweapon or implant gone wrong, maybe drugs—had wasted him away, and the uniform now hung on him like a blanket. Up close, he smelled like he'd pissed his pants.

Thinking he'd passed out, I meant to slip past him, but he suddenly stuck out one spindly leg to block my way to the front door. When I turned, his rheumy eyes were studying me.

He tried to speak, coughed a phlegmy cough, and gave it another shot. "Where do you think you're going?" he rasped.

"I'm looking for the super," I said.

"That's me. Go up and look at 2A. It's vacant. You don't need me to go with you. What are you going to steal?" He laughed, then coughed again.

Somewhere inside the tenement, on one of the upper floors by the echoing sound of it, two people started screaming at one another. Almost immediately, other voices yelled demanding that the squabbling couple shut up. The first two paid no attention, nor did the super show any sign that he thought he ought to get up and intervene.

I supposed that for my purposes, that was good. "I don't want a room," I said. "I'm trying to trace someone. I want to know if he stayed here." I showed him Victim Three's image.

He squinted while the screaming inside grew louder. "You a cop?"

I shook my head. "When was the last time you saw the police on this street? I'm a journalist. You may have seen some of my reports."

"Hell, no," he snorted. "Alright, Mr. Journalist, what's it worth to you?"

Despite that response and its implications, I wasn't excited. The man's sly manner didn't inspire confidence. "If you can tell me something about him—like his name—twenty creds. But if it turns out you lied about knowing him, I won't be happy."

He glared. "I was U.S. Marines Orbital Drop. *Regular* infantry, not armored up in a can. I was at Xiangong. I'd break you in half."

I raised a conciliatory hand. "Sorry. I spoke out of turn. I respect your service, and I'm not trying to give you a hard time. I'm just asking you to be honest."

The vet held my eye for another moment, then grunted. "The man didn't stay here. Now get the hell off my porch."

"Thank you." I started back toward the street.

A portable holodisplay plummeted in front of my face and smashed to pieces at my feet. One of the quarreling duo had thrown it out the window, and it was pure luck it hadn't smashed my head in.

I lurched around in case anything else was falling down at me—happily, nothing was—and the super cackled at what was likely the wide-eyed shock on my face. He still didn't seem to think the situation upstairs warranted his getting involved. I could only imagine how helpful he'd be if a lodger complained of a broken appliance or bedbugs.

When I got a safe distance from the flophouse, I contemplated the next tenement in line, and the one after that. They looked as decrepit and not up to code as the place I'd just been to—and could well be just as infested with dangerous tenants and indifferent supers.

Perhaps because my near-death experience had shaken something loose in my brain, it occurred to me that right after NBN had fired me, I might well have balked at renting a room in such a dump no matter how precarious my money situation was, and I'd covered some real trouble spots when working overseas. Maybe Victim Three had opted for somewhat better accommodations even though they'd burn through his credaccount faster, and that was why he'd landed in the pit at Hoyo Rojo.

Assuming I was right, there was a huge, cheap hotel most every New Angeles resident had heard of: the Gran Hotel. An establishment of thousands of decent but far-from-lavish rooms catering to budget-conscious tourists and travelers, it seemed like a place where a culture-shocked Victim Three might have holed up while he struggled to adjust to his newly reduced circumstances, and after I wolfed down some *seco de chivo* from a street vendor, it was my next stop.

The lobby was bland and utilitarian. There was nowhere to sit, no gurgling fountain or potted ferns, just empty space where people could stand in line while waiting for a desk clerk to become available. I was glad to see there was no line at the moment and that Oscar was on duty. Short and slight—desk clerks and others working similar jobs don't do heavy lifting, so Jinteki tends to design them small so they eat less—Francois-line clones all look alike down to the stereotypical little French mustache, but I recognized him from the oval brass nametag pinned to his vest.

The Gran Hotel is one of the owners that allow androids some time off. Supposedly the practice promotes their mental health while teaching them more about the world and thus making them more useful. What it had done for Oscar was give him hobbies— gardening and drinking teas from around the world—that took money to pursue. It also loosened his conditioning a little. The Gran has a policy against providing information about its guests, but questions worded with the proper circumspection and accompanied by modest bribes had gotten me what I needed before.

I said hello and showed him Victim Three on my PAD. He barely glanced at it before replying, "I'm sorry, sir. Without proper authorization, I am unable to respond to inquiries of this nature."

I frowned. That might be what management wanted him to say, but it wasn't our special code. If he'd never seen Victim Three, he should have said something on the order of, "I'm sorry, sir; I don't recognize him." If he had, the answer was supposed to be something like "It's possible, sir, but so many people come and go that I can't be certain." Then we would have danced around his conditioning from there until he'd communicated what I wanted to know.

"But I *have* authorization." I flashed him a glimpse of the credstick I held in my other hand.

"I'm sorry, sir," he repeated. "That is not a form of authorization I'm allowed to accept."

Had management noticed him straying beyond acceptable parameters and put him in the shop to have his conditioning reinforced? Or had a supervisor simply threatened him with punishment, maybe even early termination? I studied his calm, pleasant features in an effort to figure out what was really going on.

It didn't help. The trouble with cookie-cutter faces engineered and conditioned to produce a limited set of banal expressions is that they can be difficult to read, and I certainly wasn't having any luck at the moment.

"Thanks for nothing," I growled.

"Have a pleasant evening, sir," Oscar said as I turned away.

Once I got back out on the street and indulged my irritation for a few seconds—maybe Human First was onto something—I tried to come up with a plan B. I could fish around for a human being to bribe, but if there'd been a hotel-wide crackdown on employees disclosing what they shouldn't, that might not work. Hell, I might even end up trying to suborn an honest employee who refused to sell out their employer on moral grounds. There was probably one in Base de Cayambe somewhere.

Maybe it was time to get tricky again. It hadn't exactly gone according to plan in Hoyo Rojo, but never let it be said that I learn from experience.

I found a shop catering to tourists and grabbed a "Walking Tour of Base de Cayambe" map from a rack of such brochures. Next, with my vidlenses and red tie hidden away in inner pockets of my jacket, I found a side entrance to the Gran Hotel lobby and lurked there until Oscar left his station to take a break or because his shift had ended. I then went inside and booked a room.

I visited my accommodations briefly and then moved on to the bar, a quiet, dimly lit space with holoscreens displaying vid of space and spaceships as seen from a beanpod at the top of the Stalk as smooth Marz Jass playing over the speakers. I wondered fleetingly if real Martian colonists ever listened to it. For their sake, I hoped not.

I grabbed a booth, set the walking-tour map on the table before me, and tried to look lonely. The bar wasn't busy, and it only took a moment for a human waitress made up like the latest fashion ads, with neon green lipstick and shimmering silver hair, to show up and take my drink order. The look was too much, but the dim light helped, as did her cleavage. She'd left the top four buttons of her blouse undone to display it to good advantage. Her nametag read Nicole.

She spotted the map. "Seeing the sights?"

"Sort of. I was in town for sales meetings, and we finished early. My flight home isn't until tomorrow, so I figured I might as well have a look around."

"Did you have a good time?"

I shrugged. "Playing tourist isn't as much fun when you're on your own."

"That's a shame. No one should pass through Base de Cayambe without having a good time. Let me go get you that cerveza." When she came back with it, she lingered to chat some more.

Here's a secret about the Gran Hotel. One of the attractions, albeit not one you'll see featured in ads scripted to appeal to the average traveler, is the absence of seccams in the hallways.

That means there's no record of who goes in and out of the various sleeping rooms, which makes them good places for guests to conduct illegal business. But it also provides opportunities for hotel staff willing and able to take advantage of them.

I happened to know Nicole and some of the other bar staff had done exactly that. It was random information that had more or less fallen in my lap a year ago when I was chasing another story, and I'd never done anything with it. It wasn't all that titillating, revolting, or bizarre by the high standards of my particular audience.

The conversation grew gradually more and more flirtatious until the guy I was pretending to be found the nerve to ask Nicole up to his room. The invitation seemingly flustered her—she hoped I realized she was a nice girl who wouldn't do that kind of thing ordinarily, not unless she really and truly liked you—but she said yes.

When her shift ended and we went upstairs, she certainly behaved like she really and truly liked me. My body responded even though I knew matters were going to stop well short of the finish line. I guessed that was just as well considering that I didn't want her to suspect I was playing her instead of the other way around.

In due course, the door opened. The mechanism was meant to do so gently for someone it recognized as authorized to enter, but the big man on the other side didn't give it the chance. He shoved it to make it bang dramatically into the wall. I hadn't seen him before but assumed he worked elsewhere in the hotel, near enough that Nicole could depend on him to show up before the mark got her panties off.

Fists clenched, glaring, he snarled, "That's my wife!"

"Thiago!" Nicole cried, recoiling against the headboard, horrified as could be. I had to give them credit. They could both have acted in holonovelas.

"I'm going to kill you!" said Thiago, stalking toward me. Not as quickly as he could have. It wasn't that far to the bed, and he didn't want to close the distance before I collected my wits and started talking. Then he would have had to start actually roughing me up to maintain the act, and that could have taken us all off script.

Suppressing the urge to laugh, I squawked, "No! Please! I didn't know!"

"He didn't!" Nicole said.

"I don't care!" Thiago said.

"I'm sorry," I said. "Let me make it up to you. I'll pay!"

"I don't want your money!" Thiago said.

"Please!" Nicole said. "If you hurt him, you'll go to jail, and the children need you! I need you. Please!"

Thiago stood and thought about it, breathing heavily, barrel chest heaving. "How much will you pay?" he asked.

"Five hundred."

"Forget it," He took another step toward me.

"A thousand!" I clambered up from the bed and reached for my credstick where it sat atop the dresser. "Please!"

Once again, Thiago pondered. Then, reluctantly, still the very image of bloodlust barely held in check, he said, "A thousand." He told his PAD, one of the wristwatch models, "Access my credaccount."

"And, scene," I said.

Thiago blinked at me. "What?"

"We're done," I said. "You two have been running the badger game on guests who wandered into the bar. Now that you've tried to run it on me, I can prove it."

They both looked stunned. Nicole recovered first. "It's your word against ours!"

"No," I said, "I've got it all on vid. But I don't particularly want to show the world my bare ass and private parts, so let's—"

Nicole pointed. "It's there—get it!"

Damn it, now we were going off *my* script. Set to motion activation, the vidlenses were on the shelf in the closet, the closet door was open just a crack, and I'd dimmed the lights, ostensibly to create a proper atmosphere for sex. The grifters weren't supposed to spot the device doing the recording, but Nicole had.

Thiago turned and lunged for the closet. I moved to grab him, and a hundred pounds give or take landed on my back and knocked me staggering. Nicole had jumped on me, wrapped her arms around my upper torso, and now groped with yellow nails glitter-dusted with scarlet to claw my face. Her body squirming and rubbing against me didn't feel anywhere near as erotic as it had a minute ago.

I planted a foot in front of me to recover my balance, jerked my arms up, and loosened her grip. When I rammed an elbow backward into her, she gasped and fell away. I scrambled after Thiago, who'd almost made it to the closet. He heard me coming, whirled, and threw a punch.

His size and ability to convey violent intent had likely scared many a sucker, but he didn't really know how to fight. It was easy to slip the attack, catch him in an armlock, and force him down on his knees. He strained to break free, I applied a little more pressure, and he stopped.

"Are we done?" I panted.

He nodded. "Then get over there with Nicole." She was just straightening up.

As he obeyed, I felt more pleased with myself than the situation warranted. Probably I was using my sad little assertion of alpha-male dominance to prop up my ego after the humiliation I'd suffered in Hoyo Rojo, begging for my life and making a deal that knocked another chip out of my journalistic integrity, assuming I had any left.

I pulled on the vidlenses. My reflection in the dresser mirror assured me I looked sillier than usual wearing them and nothing else, but this way, I was sure I'd be able to protect them henceforth.

Meanwhile, Nicole was putting on her bra. "You assaulted us," she said. "Now *that's* recorded."

I sighed. She might be a professional, but she didn't know when to quit. "Can we please just talk this over like adults? I tried to tell you, I don't *want* to tell your bosses what you've been doing. I don't want to call the cops. I don't even want money. I just want some information and thought I might need leverage to get it."

Nicole frowned. "What do you want to know?"

"Hold on." Fairly sure the physical part of the program was over, I risked putting on my pants, then showed her Victim Three on my PAD. "Recognize him? Try to imagine him without the scabs and bruises. If he stayed here, I wouldn't be surprised if he came to the bar to drink away his troubles."

"Yeah," Nicole said. "He was here for a little. Mr. Ghazali, right?"

"You tell me," I said, feeling the excitement an investigator feels when they finally get their hands on the next piece of the puzzle. "That and everything else you know about him."

"He lost his job with some Weyland company. That meant he lost his apartment, too—his credit, pretty much everything."

I understood how that could happen. The old-fashioned tradition of the company store is alive and well in many of New Angeles' megacorps. Your organization takes care of virtually all your needs, and it can be a sweet deal unless you unexpectedly get fired. Then, if you burned through your cash pay as fast you got it like many such employees do—like I did, back in the old days—you could find yourself out on the street with nothing.

"Why did he get fired?" I asked.

"He said he didn't understand it. Look, I didn't spend a ton of time talking to him. At first, I thought he might want to take me to his room. That could have helped him forget his problems, too. Well, if it had gone the way he expected. But he didn't pick up on the hints. I think he was too upset for sex."

"So you started trolling for other marks."

"Thiago and I have to make a living. Management wants humans in certain jobs. They think the guests like it better. But the owners *would* replace us if they had to pay us a decent wage."

"I understand. You two are the *real* victims. Was there another customer that Ghazali talked to quite a bit? Or maybe just someone who came in at the same times he did? Somebody who might have been watching him?"

She shook her head. "Not that I noticed."

I tried to think of something else worth asking and came up empty. The elation of discovery was fading fast. I'd tracked down Victim Three, but had that really gotten me any closer to the killer?

I almost told my informants they could go, then, on impulse, decided to show them Victim Two as well. I had no reason to expect they'd recognize that one, but as long as they were here and so was I, why not?

"Ms. Baxter," Nicole said. "She came into the bar, too."

Damn! Maybe I was onto more than I'd thought. Nicole hadn't noticed anyone stalking Ghazali, but that didn't mean no one had. Maybe the killer was choosing *all* their victims from guests who stayed in the hotel.

"Tell me about her," I said.

"It was basically the same with her as it was with Ghazali. One of the Weyland companies let her go for no good reason, or at least that's how she saw it. It kicked her out of her apartment in her arcology and gave her the voucher as part of what passed for her severance pay."

Amazed by this new bit of information, I asked, "What voucher?"

"The voucher to stay here for a while. I guess somebody decided it would look bad to just toss a fired employee out on the street. Over the past couple months, there have been one or two other guests who ended up in the hotel the same way. Maybe even more I don't know about."

In a way, it made sense. The Weyland Consortium—well, technically, one of the zillion divisions and subsidiary companies that made up Weyland—owned the Gran Hotel like it owned all sorts of things besides the Beanstalk. If it felt like giving budget accommodations to a terminated employee for a week or two, why not use one of its own businesses?

But it would be a hell of a coincidence if the serial killer then simply happened to fixate on Ghazali *and* Baxter out of all the people coming and going in the hotel. What if, instead, the killer was hunting fired Weyland company employees specifically? God knew why that would be, but it wasn't actually impossible. I wished I had an identifiable picture of Victim One or knew anything at all about the people murdered previously.

Since I didn't, I told Nicole and Thiago we were done, and because we agreed it would be better if we weren't all seen together, I rode down on an elevator ahead of them and used my PAD to check out on the way.

Wondering what everything added up to and what my next move ought to be, I hiked away from the Gran. Humming, a dark-colored hopper floated down from a skylane above and hovered next to the curb a few feet in front of me. The rear gull-wing door lifted, and a voice at my back said, "Get in."

I turned. Before me stood the gang member with the metal arm I'd seen in Hoyo Rojo. I like to think I would have noticed him tailing me if I hadn't been lost in thought, but maybe he was just good at his job.

I considered whether it would be safer to go with my would-be abductor or make a break for it. The prosthetic answered my unspoken question by sliding open a hatch midway between wrist and elbow and extruding a small but nonetheless intimidating laser weapon.

I gave him a smile. "No need for that." I climbed into the hopper next to a second gangster. Metal Arm got in after me, so I was penned in on both sides. The door closed, and the car rose into the air.

CHAPTER 4

I wish I had a window seat," I said. "It's been a while since I've ridden in a hopper. These days, I'm more of a Metro guy."

Neither of my companions replied. So much for trying to break the ice.

"What's this all about?" I asked. "I haven't posted anything about Los Scorpiones in a while, and the last time I did, it wasn't any worse than the kind of thing I've been posting for years."

Metal Arm gave me a tiny shrug. The shoulder with the prosthetic didn't lift and drop in quite the same way as the other. "A boss tells us to pick you up, we pick you up."

"And take me where?"

"La Cocina."

That was marginally reassuring. La Cocina was one of the most popular Spanish restaurants in Base de Cayambe's Old Town. It was also a place where Los Scorpiones held meetings, both among themselves and with outsiders. It wasn't absolutely out of the question that Metal Arm and his partner were taking me there to kill me—very little was absolutely out of the question where this particular gang was concerned—but it seemed to me that if that was what they wanted, they had more private and convenient locations to use.

Clinging to that perspective, I tried to enjoy the ride. Along with anxiety, triggered memory got in the way.

Outside the windows in the jammed skylanes, countless other hoppers maneuvered among the spires, guided by the traffic control computers of the New Angeles Transit Authority. Some had headlights to make their owners feel more secure even though they serve no real function anymore; others had just multicolored accent lights to lend some style.

It's supposed to be a safe system, and by and large, it is. Only rarely does blazing wreckage plunge down on unlucky pedestrians from hundreds of feet overhead.

It was investigating an uptick in such accidents that cost me my classy well-paying job at NBN. The traffic control system only worked if the software was bug-free in both the city's computers and in all the computers of the individual hoppers, and the software in the new Gemini Motors Angel wasn't. The company was selling the cars anyway, because fixing the glitch would have been expensive and pushed back the rollout date.

Unfortunately, an executive decreed that reporting the story "wasn't in the public interest," possibly because Gemini made a payoff or called in a favor. He spiked the report, and even more unfortunately, despite my years in the business, I somehow hadn't learned when it was time to let go. I made a stink about it, got canned, and ended up videoing hookers and roaches in the undercity to make a marginal living.

The hopper set down on a charging pad attached to the La Cocina garage. Once my escorts and I got out, a zap of flash charge brought the vehicle's battery back to full capacity. The hopper then rolled into a parking cube to make way for the next hopper to arrive.

La Cocina itself is an old brick commercial building several stories tall, with the public part of the restaurant occupying the bottom three. I caught a glimpse of some of the diners on the ground floor as Metal Arm and his partner marched me to a private elevator. Smiling and chattering, silverware or beverages in their hands, they all looked like they were having a better time than I was.

I didn't know whether to feel better or worse when the gang members escorted me to a private room on the fifth floor. A woman with a face as lovely and seductive as any sensie superstar awaited me. In fact, with her black hair, brown eyes, and dark, flawless complexion, she looked rather like Carolina Mendoza, the sensie star, a resemblance for which she could likely thank a cosmetic surgeon. She had the figure of a sensie superstar, too: curvy and very fit.

She was sitting at a table laden with steaming *soya paella* and *empanadas de verde* served family style. There was a place setting in front of the empty seat opposite hers.

It was all somewhat reassuring. Providing supper wasn't an obvious prelude to violence, and I'd dealt amicably with this woman before. But it was far from *completely* reassuring, because she was Lívia Teixeira, a boss universally considered more dangerous than even the average Scorpiones member. Eschewing bodyguards as an unnecessary encumbrance, she prowled Base de Cayambe alone in a black duster that supposedly held a small arsenal of weapons. She wasn't wearing the coat at the moment, but with the unnatural strength provided by military-grade g-mods, she wouldn't need the contents should she decide to dispose of the likes of me.

"You can go," she told Metal Arm and his partner. She smiled at me. "Sit. Eat."

The thought crossed my mind that I probably should. This was a better meal than any I'd been able to afford lately. Unfortunately, though, I doubted I could eat with anxiety drying and clogging my throat. I could drink, though. In fact, it seemed like a good idea. I poured myself a glass of red wine and gulped some down.

"Barbarian," Lívia said. "La Cocina has nice *riojas*. They deserve to be savored, not guzzled."

"It's been a long day," I said. "Maybe I'll slow down next glass. Why did you want to see me?"

"So direct," she said. "I kind of like that. When most people talk to me, they take forever to get to the point. Like they're afraid that if they say one word wrong, I'll snap their neck."

"Well," I said, "to be fair…"

She laughed. "It has been known to happen. But I've calmed down now that I'm responsible for recruitment. People won't join if they're worried you'll kill them the minute the first little thing goes wrong."

"About my likably direct question…"

"Right. We know what you've been looking into."

"How?"

"Does it matter?"

Maybe it didn't, really. Though you might not guess it from my groping, floundering progress, people with abundant connections and resources—people like Los Scorpiones—have plenty of ways to obtain and correlate information. Still, I said, "It would satisfy my curiosity."

"All right; here's the short version. A lot of business gets done in the Gran Hotel. It pays us to have ears there."

"Okay, but why are you interested in *my* current business?"

"I didn't have you brought here so I could answer your questions."

"Was it so I could answer yours? Are Los Scorpiones hunting the serial killer?" If so, that could make one hell of a story.

She shook her head. "There you go again, asking something else."

"If you are hunting him, maybe we can share information. Work together. I can make Los Scorpiones look like heroes. You took a deadly maniac off the streets, did what the cops couldn't or wouldn't—"

"Stop," Lívia said. "We don't care what you think you know, because it isn't much, and we're not conducting any sort of manhunt. Who do you think Los Scorpiones are, anyway?"

So much for that theory, then. This wasn't *M* even if Lívia did look a lot like the star of the most recent sensie remake.

"Maybe you *should* be hunting him," I said. "Sooner or later, the general public is going to find out there's a sadistic killer on the loose. That could keep people away from the district and be bad for business, including stim and prostitution."

"People might never find out if you don't tell them."

I took a breath. "So that's what this is? Why? Is the killer a member? A boss? Are you protecting them? It would be smarter to cut them loose."

"You aren't listening to me. *Stop asking questions.* Right here, right now. I can make it worth your while. Money and a lead on a different story. What about some dirt on 14K? Those tri-maf bastards have some inconvenience coming to them."

"How much money?" I asked.

She told me, and it was pretty generous considering that she could have just come around the table and snapped my neck. It was enough to pay off my debts and keep me afloat for a while: long enough, if my luck would only change, for me to up my income again. Hell, maybe the 14K story would turn things around.

"All right," I said. "It's a deal."

And I more or less thought I meant it. Given the circumstances, I was certainly trying to seem like I meant it, and I thought I'd done so until Lívia's brown eyes narrowed. Apparently she sensed an underlying lack of enthusiasm.

"Do you know how many serial killers there are operating in New Angeles at any given time?" she asked.

"No," I said.

"Well, neither do I, really. But I wouldn't be surprised if there are hundreds."

"So what's another more or less?"

"For that matter, do you know how many people die ugly, early deaths across the city every day? Do you think you can save them all?"

"No."

"Do you think you can save one percent? Or one percent of one percent? Or even just one percent of one percent of one percent?"

"No."

"Of course not, because you're not an idiot. You understand you're just one little person, and the big bad world is going to be what it is no matter what you do. So the only sensible thing to do is look out for yourself."

She had a point. Pretty much every really bad thing that had happened to me in recent years, from getting fired from NBN to the beating and humiliation I'd just suffered in Hoyo Rojo, had happened because I'd insisted on jamming myself into the gears of one big machine or another.

"I'm talking to you this way," Lívia continued, "because I know you can be reasonable. Your reports on Los Scorpiones show it. Now, if you refuse to be reasonable this time…"

"I get it," I said. "I'll be good." I wasn't as afraid anymore. It seemed likely she was going to let me go unharmed. But I had a heavy feeling in my gut like I'd swallowed a chunk of lead.

Lívia smiled. "I knew I could count on you." She passed a cred-stick across the table.

CHAPTER 5

I picked up a bottle of *aguardiente* on the way back to my studio apartment—really more of an improvised recording studio–editing bay with a fold-up cot leaning against the wall and a tiny kitchenette and bathroom jammed into the back—and kept drinking. The sugar-cane liquor mixed poorly with *rioja*, and I woke at four in the morning with a foul taste in my mouth and an aching head. Fortunately, I had hangover pills on hand to get rid of all that, though they couldn't protect me from the nightmare I had when I was finally able to fall asleep again. I was running my game on Nicole like I had in real life, only suddenly she wasn't Nicole anymore. She was Lívia, and she jumped off the bed and came at me with a stiletto. I fled through endless hotel corridors with the ball and chain from Hoyo Rojo slowing me down.

It would be an exaggeration to say that a late breakfast of green plantain dumplings in the little cafeteria down the street enabled me to forget the warning implicit in the dream, but it fortified me for what was to come. When I finished, I hiked to the corner Metro station, descended four long, steep escalators, and caught the next tube-lev train headed in the direction of Jak's Workshop. The morning commuter crush was over, but an out-of-towner might not have believed it. I still had to stand with other people's bodies bumping and brushing me as the high-speed train accelerated and slowed down.

Grateful when it reached my stop, I caught an elevator up to ground level. From there, Jak's Workshop was only two blocks away.

When you first walk in the door, the Workshop can seem like any another garage, the floor littered with broken hopper parts, the walls hung with a miscellany of tools, and the place echoing with the clank of metal and the whine of power wrenches tightening or loosening lugs. On further inspection, though, you took in just how many bays there were, that there were additional cavernous spaces beyond the first one, and that racing trophies and memorabilia filled the shelves. And if you were a gearhead, you might soon register the complete competence with which the bustling mechanics, each wearing brown coveralls with a name patch reading "Jak," were doing their work.

Ignoring the "Mechanics Only Beyond This Point" sign, I walked past repair jobs in progress and other customers waiting their turn, searching for *my* Jak, a stocky, slow-moving guy whose grease- and oil-stained coveralls looked like they had never been washed since the day he put them on. As I rather expected, he wasn't out in the front portion of the garage. Conveniently, there was still no one paying attention when I wandered farther back.

To an ignoramus like me, the jobs underway there looked just like the ones out front, except perhaps, on average, more extensive. If you knew what you were looking at, though, you could tell the hoppers weren't being merely fixed but also upgraded and customized for racing or to suit the desires of their owners. Sometimes those desires were illegal. If a customer didn't smell like a cop, it was possible to get almost any modifications they might want—and can afford. Blowing the factory caps on speed and responsiveness was suicidal but also a guaranteed rush for thrill seekers and a necessity for criminals fleeing with the police in hot pursuit.

When I found my Jak, he had a hopper up on a lift and was applying the hissing blue flame of a welding torch to the undercarriage. Upon noticing me, he switched off the torch, pushed up his goggles, and gave me a look that was half-interested, half-wary. I get that look from my contacts quite a bit.

"Jak," I said. "Long time, no see."

"Zamora," he replied. "What's up?"

"I need to borrow a hopper for a few hours," I said. "It should look nice but not flashy. A middle-class family kind of car."

He grunted. "You know, there are rental places."

"That keep records. And wouldn't fix me up with a car that can talk to the city computers while feeding them a phony ID. Come on, I know you can help me out. You must have a repair job that's ready to go, but the owner told you he won't be back for it until tomorrow or the next day. Or else something boring on the outside but souped-up on the inside that the workshop is waiting to sell to the right buyer."

"If you don't get it back on time and in good condition—"

"It's your ass. I understand. That's why I'm willing to pay you well." With the credstick Lívia had given me in my pocket, I finally didn't have to worry about the cost of doing business. Not for a while, anyway.

"How well?" he asked.

After we negotiated a price, he led me to a nondescript green Gemini compact parked in the very back of the building and reprogrammed the transponder. Then I got in and gave the hopper voice commands, and a hatch in the roof immediately above it slid open. The vehicle floated straight up through the opening and onward, dodging other hoppers, elevated slidewalks, and mag-lev tracks as it ascended.

My first stop was my own apartment. I hurried in, and when I came out again, I too was a Jak. On impulse, suspecting it might come in handy someday, I'd seized the opportunity to pilfer the coveralls from a trash can in the garage three years back. When I retrieved them, they were sticky and stinking with some sort of pink spillage, but half a dozen cleanings got rid of the stain and smell.

My contact might well have balked at my masquerading as one of Jak's Workshop's mechanics. If my plan didn't work, the disguise increased the chances of my screwup coming back on him. That was why I hadn't mentioned this part of it.

I climbed back in the compact and told it to fly to my next destination. Up above the perpetual gloom, the skylanes were crowded as usual, and NATA, for its own inscrutable reasons, seemed to be prioritizing flows of traffic at right angles to my own. The result was a forty-five-minute trip that gave me time to wonder what the hell I was doing.

After all, both the cops and Los Scorpiones had warned me off. Lívia Teixeira had even offered me money to back off, and I'd taken it—not that, in the moment, I'd felt I really had a choice. There could be heavy consequences if I continued, maybe even that blade I'd dreamed about slicing my throat, and was I confident of my ability to dodge them? Absolutely not. If there was any moral to be drawn from the course of my life to date, it was that in the real world, Goliath beat David every time.

Even if somehow, some way, this time turned out to be the exception, so what? Lívia was right: Exposing the atrocities of one serial killer wasn't going to make this corrupt, miserable world a better place. If it brought fear and financial hardship to the lower levels of Base de Cayambe, it might make my little piece of the planet worse.

And it wasn't like I *needed* the story anymore. As promised, Lívia had provided a tip that would enable me to report on Mr. Li's 14K blackmailing of customs and security officials at the Beanstalk to facilitate smuggling offworld or down to us here on Earth. My viewers wouldn't be as interested as they would be in wallowing in the gory details of a serial killer's rampage, but properly packaged, the subject might pique their interest well enough.

Still, here I was, despite all the reasons not to be. Why?

Well, there was the happy fantasy that the serial-killer story would turn out to be so amazing that NBN would beg me to come back, or, failing that, that some other powerful Network company would recruit me. Restored to my former elevated position in my profession with my employer protecting its investment in me, I should be beyond the reach of Los Scorpiones. Unfortunately, though, based on what little I'd learned so far, I doubted the story would be *that* remarkable.

It was intriguing, though. The discovery that a maniac was cutting up random people in the district would have merely been sensational, but the possibility the killings *weren't* random, that the murderer was choosing victims from among former Weyland employees staying in the Gran Hotel, turned the matter into a puzzle a reporter might actually be able to solve, and puzzles like that interested me. The chance to tackle them and get paid for it was one of the reasons I'd become a journalist in the first place and no doubt a reason I was once again having trouble letting go.

Especially since my ego had gotten involved. Apparently, despite all the knocks it had taken in recent years, I still had some pride left. I didn't like knuckling under in the face of pressure, and when it was obvious the person applying it was sure I would, like Lívia had been, it made the experience all the more humiliating. It sparked the reckless urge to demonstrate, if only to myself, that I hadn't *really* capitulated after all.

So here I was, resolved to probe a little deeper even if I ultimately decided this was a story I could never tell. I wasn't going to go right back to poking around in the undercity, though, where Los Scorpiones were all too likely to notice. I wasn't *that* reckless. I was going to come at the story from the other end up here above the plaza level.

Not that this approach would be completely safe, either. Megacorps can be as secretive about their internal affairs and as unwelcoming to prying outsiders as any gang, and the Weyland Consortium has a reputation for being more secretive than most. But they had no reason to be on the lookout for me and, even if they caught me, *probably* wouldn't kill me out of hand.

Many of the countless Weyland companies have their executive offices in the Watts-Watson Industrial Solutions Tower, and Weyland proper runs some of its administrative functions out of it as well. (For those keeping score, WWIS is owned by Skyline Investments, which is in turn owned by Weyland.) The colossal structure is an ugly concoction of boxes with blades sticking out of them stacked haphazardly into a pile. Or, if you like that sort of thing, it's a breathtaking example of contemporary architecture. Connected to it by slidewalks and little maglev lines is the Midas Arcology, where its employees live. The WWIS Tower looms over Midas, though the latter is enormous in its own right.

In the penthouses perched at the top of the arcology, top management reportedly lives in palatial style. But after my years dwelling in the shadows of the undercity with the crumbs and trash of the plaza level drifting down on my head, even the apartments lower down, with their balconies, gleaming windows, and convenient access to amenities like swimming pools and tennis courts, looked nice enough to elicit a wistful pang in me.

Beyond the arcology, palatial and nice give way to construction sites and utilitarian temporary housing for android and human laborers. Watts-Watson Industrial Solutions has bought up pretty much the whole Neo-Broadway area and demolished everything that once stood there. I believe I've already mentioned how much we New Angelinos cherish the cultural heritage of old Ecuador.

I'd considered asking about Victims Two and Three—Baxter and Ghazali—in the Midas Arcology. They *might* have lived there, but not necessarily. The Weyland companies provide plenty of worker housing elsewhere. Even if they had lived in Midas, I still would have needed to track down neighbors who'd actually known them among the thousands of residences.

Thus I was headed for the WWIS building, even though I was certain security was even tighter there. Acting as instructed, my borrowed Gemini flew on past a place where the top executives park—the unassuming little compact would have been out of place amid the Qianjus and other luxury hoppers, and nobody who owned one of those would have patronized Jak's Workshop—and floated down to a rooftop where lesser beings put their cars.

That didn't mean security was any less stringent. Camdrones—or, if you prefer, gundrones; these were both—buzzed around the hopper as it descended. By the time it lit on the charging pad, topped off its battery, and rolled away to a regular parking cube, a guard in a black, glossy body-armor vest, and with an Argus Model 19 pistol holstered on one hip and an electric truncheon hanging on the other, was headed in my direction. Drawing what encouragement I could from the fact that he didn't appear to be in any particular hurry, I took a deep breath and climbed out of the vehicle with PAD in hand.

The legend on the guard's cuirass told me his name was BANERJEE. He didn't bother asking mine. Maybe he figured that, as the annoying workplace affectation dictated, I'd just answer "Jak." Instead, he wanted to know my "business."

"The customer works in the building," I said. "He wanted us to drop the hopper off here when we got it fixed."

"What's the customer's name?" Banerjee asked.

I looked at the PAD, currently displaying what I hoped was a convincing imitation of a Jak's Workshop work order. "Rodriguez."

"First name?"

I looked at the PAD again. "It doesn't say. Maybe Jak was in a hurry, and he knew the guy, or something."

The guard frowned. "Do you know how many Rodriguezes work here?"

Technically, no, but I was betting it was a lot. New Angeles is the cosmopolitan crossroads of the solar system, but it still has more South American residents than any other kind, and according to the last world census, the most common surname on the continent is Rodriguez. That being the case, the Weyland companies almost certainly employed plenty of them, too many for the security guard to relish the prospect of calling department after department until he found the right guy.

"Look," I said, "you don't need to find him. He doesn't have to sign anything. This is Hopper Pad 371-G, right?"

"Yeah."

"Well, this is where he told us to bring the car, and this is where he'll come looking for it. Another hopper is coming to pick me up and take me back to the garage."

Banerjee stood and thought about it, I hoped following the trail I'd laid out for him. The drones and seccams had scanned the vehicle, and it was harmless. Unarmed, and so was I. He still wasn't supposed to let me into the building without the proper ID or authorization, but then, I wasn't *trying* to get in. I just needed to hang around on the roof until my ride showed up.

"Fine," Banerjee said. Turning away, he looked at his own wristwatch PAD and the data streaming from the drones as they inspected another hopper descending on the charging pad. He didn't get excited, so I inferred the new one wasn't a bomb-carrying juggernaut of destruction, either.

I wandered over to a shelter provided for people waiting to be picked up like I supposedly was, sat down, and tried to look bored and a little impatient. A couple minutes before three, I went into the restroom and took possession of a stall. A few minutes past, I came out again to see that, as expected, the shift had changed and new guards were on duty.

Affecting an air of casual confidence, I strode toward the doors that led into the building. With its scanners, instant lockdown capability, and pop-up barricades currently just barely visible as grey-on-grey rectangles in the floor, the entrance looked as hard to breach as the entrances to the Base de Cayambe precinct building. Maybe harder.

A guard whose vest read FERNANDEZ planted herself in my path. "Where do you think you're going?" she asked.

I gave her a quick look at the phony work order. "I need for Mr. Rodriguez to sign off on this, and then I need to bring him up here and show him the hopper if he wants to make sure everything's okay. Mr. Banerjee said it was all right."

"Then why didn't he pass you in?"

"I wanted to use the bathroom first." I gave her a sheepish smile. "It was kind of an emergency."

She frowned, deliberating, and once again, I *hoped* I could guess what was going on in her head. I looked like a Jak. The drones and such had scanned me and decided I wasn't carrying anything dangerous. The seven-to-three shift must have assessed me and found nothing amiss, or else I wouldn't be wandering around on the rooftop in the first place. She *could* check with Banerjee, but he wouldn't like being bothered when he was already off the clock any more than she would have herself.

Fernandez gave me a VISITOR badge to stick to my coveralls. "Go on in."

Though it was irrational, I felt a twinge of anxiety as I passed through a final scan on my way in, like it was going to penetrate my Jak disguise and announce to all and sundry that I was really a sleazy sensation-monger with journalistic pretensions. Fortunately, it didn't, and the double doors swung open before me.

Inside, though there was no shortage of private offices and closed doors, many spaces were open and airy. Holos, models, and stillframes of the Beanstalk were everywhere, but I also spotted representations of orbital spacecraft construction, helium-3 mining on the Moon, undersea fish farming, suits being sewn in an automated factory, and clones in paper hats serving customers at the counter of a Hungry Steve's burger franchise, the miscellany a testament to all the different businesses Weyland has a hand in.

Humans, clones, bioroids, and robots less human in design and driven by old-fashioned circuitry instead of optical brains worked industriously at their various assignments, layering 3D schemata and blueprints, video conferencing, or picking up litter, dusting, vacuuming, or polishing floors. Muted though it was, the hum the cleaning produced, or perhaps the tang of the chemicals employed, visibly annoyed a few people trying to concentrate in the immediate vicinity. Unfortunately for their nerves, the cleaners couldn't perform their duties after everyone left, because these offices operate at full capacity twenty-four seven.

It's impossible to miss the differences between this complex and NBN's, where every endeavor is about the creation of media. But the stylishly dressed and coiffed workers, the expensive interior design, the state-of-the-art technology and, yes, the cleanliness are much the same. I hadn't been in a workplace like this since my termination, and like seeing the Midas Arcology from the air, the experience evoked in me bittersweet memories and just plain bitter envy of those around me.

I closed my eyes for a second and pushed the feeling away. I needed to focus. With luck, Fernandez wouldn't worry if I didn't come back to the hopper pad right away. Rodriguez could be in a meeting, on a call, or otherwise tied up. Yet even so, it would be a bad idea to linger longer than necessary.

Unless you want to infiltrate one of the rumored top-secret basement labs, the WWIS building is like NAPD headquarters. The trick is getting in, not moving around once you are. But that was only my first problem solved. As a Jak, I had no hope of getting what I came for.

Accordingly, I found another restroom stall and stripped off the coveralls. I had on a leftover suit from my NBN days underneath. Company property; I'd stolen it on my way out. It was a little out of style and not as nice as what a number of the people working in the building were wearing, but it was the best I had and would have to do. Standing on the toilet seat, ignoring the commode's polite verbal request that I get down, I shifted a ceiling tile and stuffed the coveralls into the space above.

Now I needed a badge that would exert some authority. I wandered the open work areas until I came across several well-dressed people sitting around an oval projection table. They were studying and discussing a holographic chart that changed from one moment to the next as vertical bars jumped up and down and the diagonal lines connecting data points shifted. I had no idea what the display represented. The stock market, maybe?

I didn't really care. What mattered to me was that some of the chairs around the table were empty, a man had draped his blazer over the back of the one next to him, and his badge was stuck on the breast pocket. I ambled up behind the seat and, trying to look like I was kibitzing and hoping my mediocre pickpocket skills were up to this new challenge, peeled the badge off the jacket and slipped it in my pocket. The holodisplay helped. It blocked the view of the people on the other side of the table.

By the time I finished, puzzled faces were turning in my direction. I put on my sheepish expression again. "Sorry. I thought this was the meeting I'm supposed to be in." I walked away before anybody could ask what meeting that was.

I glanced at a wall monitor that displayed, among other information, the time. Fourteen minutes had passed since I'd infiltrated the building. It wasn't a lot of time, really, but it felt like more, enough to quicken my pulse and spark a sudden urge to get out while I still could. I took a breath and told myself that if I just stuck to my half-assed plan, everything would work out.

The same monitor offered a searchable directory of the entire gigantic building. Rather than hike nearly the entire length of the place, I caught a little internal train that ran back and forth, then took an elevator two hundred floors up to what I hoped would prove to be the proper section of the uber–HR department that oversees HR operations in all the Weyland subsidiary companies.

Another big open classroom-like space held rows of mostly vacant computer terminals—or the spindly bare bones of them; many aspects of the peripherals were virtual—but I was leery of trying to use one myself. With my pilfered badge and the ID chip therein, I might be able to log into the database, but I wasn't confident of being able to navigate the system in a reasonable length of time once I did. I wanted help.

The scatter of mostly young people who were using the terminals all wore badges that read TRAINEE. One of them, a skinny, frowning woman with hair pulled back so tight it looked like it ought to hurt, was sitting apart from the others, maybe so their occasional murmured exchanges wouldn't distract her. Her isolation and intense, frazzled air pulled me over to her.

"Are you *still* working on that?" I snapped.

She jumped and twisted around in her seat. "Uh, yes, sir." She hesitated. "The case studies are complicated."

"They shouldn't be," I replied, "not for anyone qualified to work here."

She winced. A white-collar job in a megacorporation probably hadn't been her childhood dream, but it was her best shot at a life free from the poverty and desperation I saw in the undercity every day. "I'm qualified," she said. "I promise I am. I'll get it."

"Let me see your progress." I peered over her shoulder at the projected display before her. As near as I could make out, she was applying an algorithm to determine if some fictional employee had been abusing their sick time. I grunted as if finding fault with her work. "All right. You need a refresher. Let's take you through some basic operations."

This time when she winced, it was with a hint of resentment in the tightening of her mouth. If I insisted on drilling her on things she'd already mastered, it would only delay her completion of today's assignment. But she didn't want to antagonize me, so she went along. "Yes, sir. Thank you."

"Sometime in the last six months, a woman named Baxter working here in New Angeles was terminated. Pull up her file."

Yevtukh hesitated. "Sir, trainees are only supposed to work in practice mode except for when Mr. Widjaja tells us to go into the real data."

I gathered Mr. Widjaja was her class's trainer. Damn him for doing his job properly.

I sighed. "Really? That's your attitude? I'm willing to spend time helping you, but you're not willing to do a little extra work to acquire the skills you need?"

"Please, sir, it's got nothing to do with my attitude—"

"Don't worry about it…" I made a show of inspecting her badge. "Ms. Yevtukh. Go back to what you were doing." Turning away, I pulled my PAD out as if to make a note of her full name so I could post a comment in her file when I got around to it.

"Wait," she said. "Please. If you're telling me to, then I suppose it's all right. I mean, of course it's all right. And I do want any help you're willing to give."

If I were a nicer person, I would have felt guilty for bullying her. Actually, I did, a little, but mostly I was eager to see what she could pull up for me.

"Fine," I growled as though now regretting taking an interest in her. "Woman named Baxter. Worked here in New Angeles. Terminated within the past six months."

Like other skilled data techs I'd met, Yevtukh took advantage of every input modality. She typed on the virtual keyboard projected on the desktop before her, murmured verbal instructions, and used blink commands like the ones I employed to operate my vidlenses. In just a few seconds, the face of the woman I'd encountered as a corpse—almost the top half of a corpse, really—in the precinct house morgue appeared before me.

"Is that her?" Yevtukh asked.

"Yes." In the moment, I nearly forgot that the guy I was impersonating had no reason to be especially excited about it. He needed to continue acting grudging and generally pissy. "Scroll through her basic information."

Yevtukh hesitated. Anyone who'd been hired for her job, anyone in the world, really, could scroll through a basic text-based data field, so how could my instruction possibly help her learn anything? It was stupid if not downright insulting. Still, she swallowed whatever she probably wanted to say and humored me.

Peering over her shoulder, I scanned the information. I wished I could capture the images with my PAD to study later, but that would have been way too peculiar. If there was a clue there, I needed to pick up on it right then.

Victim Two had been Susan Baxter. Single, no children, Canadian immigrant. Until her eviction, had lived on the ninety-second floor of the Regal Arcology. Had worked in marketing on ad campaigns for Anti-Cal Fit Shakes and Pastries. Reason for termination was "Redundancy," which could have been code for anything.

What did it all add up to beyond the obvious? Nothing was jumping out at me.

A fresh twinge of anxiety reminded me time was passing. "Keep that information handy," I told Yevtukh, "and call up the file on an employee named Ghazali. He also worked in New Angeles and was terminated within the past six months."

In another few seconds, Yevtukh had Victim Three displayed. He'd been a good-looking man before getting beaten up in Hoyo Rojo and murdered thereafter.

His full name was Nabil Ghazali. Divorced, no children, immigrant from the Middle East. Prior to his dismissal, lived on the eighty-third floor of the Hanging Gardens Arcology and was a safety inspector in the mag-lev train stations below the Root, the foundation of the Beanstalk. Also fired for "Redundancy."

Again, so what? I had Yevtukh display the files side by side and looked for common threads. Baxter and Ghazali hadn't been neighbors, nor was there any reason to think they'd ever crossed paths living in different buildings and performing their very different duties working for very different Weyland companies. Both *had* come to New Angeles from far away and evidently had no family hereabouts, which possibly explained why no one had taken them in when they unexpectedly lost their incomes and homes.

I guessed it was something, but it certainly wasn't enough. "Show me the details of the terminations," I said.

It turned out that Weyland as a whole had a pilot cost-cutting program overseeing many of its divisions and subsidiaries. The program identified employees who might be doing an adequate job but whom their companies could spare and whose elimination would save it a cred or two. My hunch was that the firings were also supposed to scare the remaining employees into working harder.

"What specific individual in the Redundancy Prevention Program tagged Baxter and Ghazali for termination?" I asked.

It only took an instant for Yevtukh to pull up the answer. "Someone named Elena Nunez signed off on both. Maybe she picked them from the start?"

"Show me her file."

Yevtukh gave me a quick sidelong glance that proclaimed my requests were getting stranger by the minute. But she still wanted to avoid a write-up in her own file and did as instructed.

Elena Nunez was a woman in her thirties with the almost fluorescently bright mismatched eyes—one blue, one green—in fashion that year. That one attempt at high style looked out of place in a round, plain, frowning face untouched by other cosmetic procedures or even makeup. Her eyebrows were a shade darker than her mousy brown hair.

Divorced, a New Angeles native, she'd grown up in a well-to-do family in the upscale Rutherford District and seemed to be enjoying a successful career in Weyland's administration, with five promotions since her employment started. If she'd ever had any problems on the job or undergone a psychological evaluation that hinted she might be a serial killer or a serial killer's accomplice, the information wasn't in any portion of her file that a lowly trainee could access.

Maybe I was chasing shadows. Coincidences that didn't mean a thing. Still, I wasn't ready to give up quite yet, even with time gnawing at my nerves. I had Yevtukh expand the files on Baxter and Ghazali section by section and tried to absorb the information that hadn't made it into the front-page summaries.

That was a daunting quantity of data. Tapped into every aspect of their employees' lives, Weyland companies have the ability to amass information on all of it, and they do. Education, work, and purchasing histories; other financial transactions; dietary and entertainment preferences; hobbies, group affiliations, and socialization matrices; pretty much anything you can imagine was available for my perusal. It was my good luck that "Medical" came up relatively early when a person was paging through.

"Shit," I said.

Eyes narrowed, a crease at the top of her nose, Yevtukh looked around at me. "I see it too," she said, "but—"

"Don't worry about it," I said. "Just do what I tell you. Can you call up a list of everyone Ms. Nunez fired in the past six months?"

"I guess so." She did. There were five thousand and ten.

"Now pick out the ones that have these characteristics." I specified the attributes Baxter and Ghazali had shared in common.

"Got them." There were twenty-seven.

Twenty-seven was only a sliver of five thousand and ten, but maybe that was helpful. Include those firings among thousands of others, and it would make it more difficult for anyone to suspect there'd been anything sketchy about them in particular.

I got lost mulling over the possibilities for a moment. When I came out of it, Yevtukh was peering at me and now looked more suspicious than intimidated.

"You weren't just training me, were you?" she asked.

I tried being Mr. Pissy one more time. "Of course I was. Your job requires you to efficiently retrieve any data a superior requires."

"If this is about a wrongful-termination lawsuit or something like that, and you tricked me into helping you—"

"Keep your voice down!" I lowered my own to a whisper. "Look, you caught me. I'm not exactly who you thought I was, but I *do* work for the company. This is an internal audit, one I'm conducting in such a way that certain employees can't find out about it prematurely and cover their tracks. Don't tell anyone, or upper management won't be happy with either of us. Whereas if you keep quiet until I'm done, I can put in a very good word for you with your department head."

I hoped she'd see that whether or not I was telling the truth, staying mum was the safe play. If I was what I claimed to be, it was to her advantage to cooperate. If I wasn't, she could get fired for showing me confidential information even if she subsequently reported the breach.

"All right," she said, somewhat dubiously, I thought. "I understand."

I took one last look at Baxter and Ghazali's medicals, trying to fix esoteric specifications and other jargon-laden information in my layman's memory. Then I took my leave of Yevtukh and walked away, trying not to look like I was hurrying.

That was hard, because I was now worried about her and Fernandez both. She still might decide to report me, after all, especially if it occurred to her that I hadn't been wearing the right kind of badge for the auditor I'd claimed to be or that such a person almost certainly wouldn't need the help of a trainee to explore the database.

But apparently she didn't rat me out, because I made it back to the train without any alarms blaring or anyone trying to stop me. No one else was in the car, which gave me the opportunity to recite what I'd memorized into my PAD. If I got caught, I'd just created a piece of evidence to prove I'd been up to no good, but I doubted building security would need any confirmation, and I didn't want to risk the information getting garbled in my head.

There weren't any guards waiting for me when I got off the train, either. Feeling increasingly confident, I strode onward. In my eagerness to escape, I almost didn't notice the group I glimpsed from the corner of my eye, the several people peering under a table or looking under the objects they'd set on top of it. Then I realized they were the same people whose meeting I'd intruded on. The guy whose badge I'd stolen had missed it, and now everyone was trying to find it.

Of course, the badge had electronics in it that would prevent it being lost or misplaced for long. In another moment, the owner was going to ping it, and I'd better not have it in my possession when that happened. Feeling horribly visible and conspicuous, I peeled the ID off my jacket and tossed it onto the floor near a coffee, juice, and snack station, a location I hoped its owner had visited at least once in the course of the day.

Nobody appeared to notice. Heart pounding, I returned to the restroom, put the Jak's Workshop coveralls back on, and headed out onto the roof.

"Hey!" Fernandez called.

I wanted to bolt the remaining distance to the Gemini. Insisting to myself that everything was still okay, I made myself stop and turn to face her instead. "Yeah."

"Did you get everything taken care of?"

"No," I said. "That idiot Jak forgot to do one thing. I have to take the hopper back to the shop to get it taken care of."

"That's annoying. But anyway, I need the VISITOR badge back."

"Right. Sorry." I returned it, climbed into the compact, and told it where to take me.

I didn't relax and slump in my seat until the hopper flew out of Neo-Broadway. Only then did I truly believe I'd infiltrated the WWIS building and gotten away clean. The relief and the pleasure I took in my own half-assed cleverness lasted until it occurred to me that I now had to decide what to do next.

I resolved to snoop for a few hours more, if only to convince myself I wasn't some spineless creature who'd cravenly obey any order Los Scorpiones gave him. But the hell of it was, I'd actually found the next piece of the puzzle; or anyway, I thought I had. Could I quit if I really was closing in on the answers?

I was half-disgusted with myself to realize that despite the excellent reasons for doing so, I couldn't. Other people had brains enough to walk away from trouble. Why didn't I? It wasn't like I *really* thought pressing on would get me my old job. On some level, I realized that was a long shot at best.

Maybe I'm no better than a junkie, and secrets are my stim or Blue Tears. I'd just had a fix but was already looking forward to the next one. Or maybe I have a death wish. Or…hell, who really knows why they do anything?

In the end, I got past the feeling that I was about to do something really, really stupid by reminding myself that even if I uncovered the whole story, I still wouldn't have to report it if I deemed it wiser not to. Such being the case, surely—for the tricky guy who'd just outwitted WWIS security—going back on a promise to Lívia Teixeira, even in the undercity, wouldn't be *too* dangerous.

CHAPTER 6

Besides tempting me to keep pursuing things a prudent person wouldn't, my visit to the plaza level was bad for me in another way. Over the years, I'd gotten used to the gloom, grime, and decay of the undercity, but my little field trip reversed that, at least briefly. The night felt darker; the neon signs, holodisplays, and fluorescent graffiti more garish; the litter and overflowing garbage more ubiquitous and malodorous; the stim dealers, wylders, streetwalkers, and panhandlers more unpredictable.

Sneering at my own jumpiness, my own foolishness, I did my best to shake the anxiety off. By the time I arrived at Sugar's Clinic, I felt more like a streetwise resident of the lower levels again, not that it was much of a happy way to feel.

The entrance to Sugar's is in a filthy, narrow alleyway. The only sign is a red neon cross in the window, the symbol harder to decipher now that a couple of the tubes that make it up have stopped glowing. Once you go inside, though, things look more promising. The interior is brightly lit and spotlessly clean, with the smell of antiseptics tingeing the air. Sugar's several medical certificates, all legitimate, hang prominently on the walls. The only thing that might put you off is that the whole place is a single room without so much as curtains to screen off one area from another. On a previous visit, I'd seen Sugar and her bioroid nurse performing gory thoracic surgery while half a dozen onlookers blanched, cringed, and tried not to puke in the waiting area just a few steps away.

That wasn't the case this time. No one was awaiting or receiving treatment, although I must not have missed the last patient by much. The bioroid, a Florence identifiable by the old-fashioned nurse's-cap shape incorporated into the contours of her head, was pulling a bloody sheet off the operating table. Pacing, Sugar Blanc was dictating notes that some mic somewhere presumably was picking up.

Sugar's a small, thin woman with a restless, get-to-the-damn-point manner that rarely goes away except when she's tending a patient. Though I didn't know the details, I could imagine why she hadn't lasted at the several hospitals that had let her go. Scowling at the interruption, or just on general principles, she said, "Pause notes. You look all right, Zamora. What is it, STI? There's no treatment for a couple of the new strains. The genitals rot right off."

"Thanks for putting that image in my head," I replied. "I don't need medical attention. I need medical info in the form of your professional opinion. If I show you some images, will you tell me what you think?"

"Are you planning to pay like for any other office visit?"

"What if I told you that you might be helping to save lives? Wouldn't the Hippocratic Oath kick in?"

"When Hippocrates starts covering my bar tab, he can talk to me about waiving my fees."

I grinned. "That's the Sugar your patients know and love. Yeah, I'll pay. I'm doing okay right now."

"You must have gotten vid of something unusually disgusting."

"You tell me." I'd downloaded the morgue vid onto my PAD, and I offered it for her inspection.

Her grouchy manner dropped away as, taking her time and pulling in tight for close-up views of the wounds, she inspected each victim in turn. Finally she asked, "Can I link to my system?"

"Sure." I told the PAD, "Let the doctor download the vid of Victims Two and Three."

She gave the corresponding command to whatever AI was listening and afterward conjured a holo of Baxter's body floating in midair.

"How did it do that?" I asked.

"It's extrapolating from what you gave it. The process would be more reliable if you'd known what angles and...skip it. Shut up and let me work."

At her command, the AI flipped the holo over for a view of its back I'd never gotten in reality. Next, she dissected the image layer by layer, system by system, and after that produced enlarged holos of the various wounds and subjected each to the same sort of methodical, in-depth examination. When the first virtual autopsy concluded, she called forth Ghazali's phantom cadaver and gave it the same painstaking treatment.

Finally, she turned to face me again. "What have I been looking at?" she asked.

"Theoretically, the handiwork of the serial killer running amok in Base de Cayambe."

"I haven't heard about that, but anyway, why 'theoretically?'"

"Both victims had some unusual health problems: the kind that, if you're lucky enough to be on a megacorporation's health insurance plan, get fixed with very expensive g-modded or mechanical transplants. I'll show you." I called up that information on the PAD. "Can you tell me if any of this stuff was left inside the bodies?"

"Hm." Ignoring my impatience or maybe even enjoying it, Sugar gave each holo what I was pretty sure was an unnecessary additional inspection. Eventually she said, "The transplants are gone. They aren't the only organs that are, but the killer definitely removed every trace of them."

"Somebody did a good job of making it look like they hacked up the bodies in a frenzy. But did they, really? Can you tell if, when they dug down to the transplants, they were careful to take them all out in one piece?"

"Removing them intact is tricky. If they were just a psychopath taking souvenirs, if they didn't know what they were doing, more likely than not, they would have left some bits and pieces behind." She hesitated a tick. "So this is about organ grinding?"

"Do you really want to know?"

"Los Scorpiones?" It was an easy guess. The gang might make more money from stim than any other source, but organ grinding was a racket for which they were particularly infamous.

I shrugged.

"Damn, Zamora! And you involve *me*?"

"There's no way it will come back on you."

"You don't know that!" She scowled. "Tell me the whole thing."

She'd helped me out a number of times before this. Maybe she had a right to know. Or maybe, deep down, I was simply itching to tell somebody.

"Standard transplant material, whether organic or mechanical, is getting cheaper and more available all the time, right?"

"Yes."

"So, while there's still money to be made stealing people's normal organs, the profit margin is shrinking. If I were a boss in Los Scorpiones, I'd want to steal the super-expensive high-end stuff designed to fix Fedorov syndrome and other terrible new diseases or make the body perform better than nature allows. Make sense?"

"I suppose."

"The problem," I said, "is that in Base de Cayambe, you've only got two sources for that kind of product. One is g-modded soldiers and spacers on leave. The other is solid citizens who live above the plaza level. Snatch either, and you might bring heat down on you that even badasses like Los Scorpiones would rather avoid."

"But considering they've got the cops in their pocket..."

"They can only count on that understanding within limits. Enough pressure from the right influential quarter, and the police will have to act regardless. Or if they don't, maybe military police or some megacorp's private security force will.

"But here's how you finesse the problem," I continued. "You partner up with an HR person *in* a megacorp. Someone pretty high up. Someone who actually has the specific job of weeding out employees who aren't needed. With access to the database, that person can identify people with the right kind of transplants, people without savings, people without family in New Angeles to take them in or miss them when they disappear. Then the HR person makes sure they're included among the firings and lets Los Scorpiones know they're going down to the undercity. The HR person even gives the targets vouchers to stay in the Gran Hotel to make sure the gang will be able to find them with a minimum of effort."

Sugar nodded. "And then the harvesters try to hide the reason for the murder by making the victims' corpses look like they simply had the bad luck to run into some bloodthirsty maniac."

"'Bloodthirsty maniac' is a pretty good description of a fair number of Los Scorpiones members, but yeah."

"Well, it's an interesting theory. It might make a good sensie. But do you have any real proof?"

"No. At this point, it's all just circumstantial." I hesitated an instant while I tried to figure out how to be tactful. "Look, you do transplants. The organs have to come from somewhere. Maybe you've already heard or seen something that could help me."

Her glare reminded me tact wasn't my strong suit. "Screw you, Zamora! I harvest organs from patients who die on me. They give permission when they sign the release. And yes, I may have some under-the-table arrangements with attendants in hospital morgues and funeral parlors. But I don't do business with organ grinders!"

I raised my hands in a conciliatory gesture. "Okay. I was just asking."

She made a little spitting sound. "You think everybody's dirty one way or another."

"You don't?"

Her lips quirked in one of her rare, fleeting, little smiles. "You've got me there. All right, I've satisfied your curiosity to the extent I'm able. Now are you going to do the sensible thing and drop this?"

"I don't know. Maybe. I keep thinking I'll run into a dead end and have no choice but to drop it, but so far..." I shrugged.

"Coming from you, that amounts to a no. Do you know why you aren't willing to let it go?"

"Tell me, Dr. Freud."

"You identify with the victims. They were unfairly cast out of the good life, and so were you. So was I. It's how I know the feeling when I see it. But we *shouldn't* identify with them. God knows, nobody from the plaza level cares about us. We belong to the undercity now, and if you're going to stick your neck out for anybody, it should be your own kind."

I mulled that over for a second. "Well, like you said to me, it's an interesting theory." I took out Lívia's credstick. "What do I owe you for the consultation?"

CHAPTER 7

Two nights later, I was shooting a human-bioroid live sex show. I still couldn't let go of what I'd come to think of as the organ-grinding story, but I thought if I obtained and posted my usual kind of content while I chased it, maybe that would reassure any member of Los Scorpiones who happened to check up on me.

Maybe I was even reassuring myself that I was back to business as usual. The organ-grinding story was just a hobby pursued for my own satisfaction, and that being the case, I wasn't going to come to harm because I hadn't walked away.

Besides, it made for a relaxing change that while shooting the sex show, I didn't have to hide my intentions. The owner of the shabby little theater in the round was glad to have me record. It was free advertising.

It soon became clear that the bioroid was impressively well equipped for the task at hand. I was trying to convince myself a winning personality was what mattered—and that I had one—when a blinking green dot appeared in the upper-right corner of my visual field. The vidlenses were letting me know I had a call.

I blinked the command to answer, and the voice of Fernando Lozano, a panhandler with a Pixel habit, rasped in my ear.

"I've got her," he said.

"You're sure?"

"Right eye blue, left eye green, right? She's waiting to catch a southbound train."

I could hardly believe my crappy plan was working. "Stay on her, and keep me updated on your location. I'm coming to meet you." I jumped up from my aisle seat and rushed up the stairs toward the exit.

Trying to figure out the logical next step in my investigation, I'd decided to focus on Elena Nunez. She had to confer with Los Scorpiones periodically, and I was betting she did it in person. The gang preferred it that way, partly to avoid leaving any sort of electronic trail in the Net and partly because, should intimidation be required, it tended to be more effective face to face on its home turf.

If I could catch Nunez having one of those meetings, maybe I could nail down proof my theory was true and answer a lingering question at the same time. What was a well-paid plaza-level executive like Nunez doing in bed with undercity lowlifes like Los Scorpiones in the first place?

The problem was *how* to catch her. As I've mentioned, Base de Cayambe is a big place.

If she traveled back and forth in a personal hopper, I was screwed, but maybe she wouldn't want NATA logging where she went and when. Even if she took a cab, the hopper service would keep a record of the trip.

No, if she truly wanted to travel anonymously, she'd use the Metro like us *plebeyos*. The Midas Arcology has its own special station where security keeps out the likes of me, but the shuttles simply take people to and from stops in the general public system.

Assuming my inferences were correct, that meant I had a shot at spotting Nunez while she was catching a public train. Luckily, I numbered beggars, grifters, and buskers who worked the Metro stations among my network of informers. I only had to let them know what I needed and that I was willing to pay for the help.

It took more time than I expected to catch up with Fernando and Nunez. She switched trains a couple times in a way that made no sense unless she was making an amateurish attempt to ensure she wasn't followed. That required me to switch trains, too.

Each stop and transfer was another chance to bail, and I wondered why the hell I didn't. My current behavior seemed particularly ill-advised given that if I was right, it was going to bring me back into proximity with Los Scorpiones, even though I fervently hoped they wouldn't notice me.

Was Sugar correct? Did my fixation on the story come from still believing deep down that people like Baxter and Ghazali were *my* people? If so, then it was snobbery driving me and a particularly pathetic variety considering that, as Sugar also told me, I was a citizen of the undercity now.

Maybe she was right to a degree. I took what comfort I could from the thought that, even if she was, there was more to it. Then, as the train pulled into the station where I would finally be able to rendezvous with Fernando, I forgot about the whole thing. The nice thing about an obsession is that when you get the chance to act on it, uncomfortable self-examination loses its hold on you.

I pulled off the vidlenses and red tie and stuffed them in my pockets before the car door dinged open, then hurried out, along the platform, and up the escalators with a rudeness that surely annoyed those I jostled in the process. I caught up with Fernando, a lanky scarecrow of a man with pockets full of the lollipops he "sold" to those he accosted, in the concourse just below ground level.

He pointed to a conservatively dressed brown-haired woman several meters ahead. She was walking briskly toward another set of escalators, so I could only see her from the back.

"You're sure?" I asked.

"One eye blue, one eye green, right?"

Nunez and plenty of other women that season, but whomever he'd followed, she was getting farther away by the second. There was no time to do anything but trust that he'd found the right person. "Let me pay you," I said, pulling Lívia's credstick out of my pocket.

He fumbled a stick out of his own jacket. Technically speaking, unnecessary, but he wasn't going to be satisfied until he verified I'd really transferred the money. It's how we do things in the undercity. "Want me to stay with you?"

"No, I've got it from here." I headed after Probably Nunez. She was already stepping onto one of the escalators up, and the urge to keep rushing and bumping people was almost irresistible. But I was close enough now that she might notice a commotion at her back.

I lost sight of her when she stepped off the top of the escalator, and when I made it up to ground level, I cast about to find her again. We'd come up in a busy patch of Mercado Baja, and the milling crowds of shoppers and entertainment seekers, the dazzling holoscreen and neon, the calls of barkers and vendors, and the blaring music of several different genres all felt like they were working together to addle and thwart me.

They didn't, though. I spotted my quarry just as she was disappearing behind a stall selling Korean barbecue. The smell of the smoke made my mouth water when I came close enough.

Reminding myself that Nunez had never met me and had, I hoped, no reason to suspect anyone was shadowing her, I decided to get a look at the brown-haired woman's face and make sure she was who she was supposed to be. Now trusting the myriad distractions of Low Market to work to my advantage, I risked maneuvering to a position from which I could see her face.

And by God, she was really Nunez. Pixel plays hell with your senses, but Fernando hadn't imagined seeing her, nor had he conned me to score money for his next fix.

Despite the tailored yet drab business suit that branded her a resident of the plaza level, Nunez strode through the market with a confidence that suggested she was either oblivious to the predators watching her pass or believed herself protected against muggers, pickpockets, and their ilk. As I allowed her to draw ahead of me again, I hoped it was the latter.

In due course, she went into the Far Frontier Poker Palace, which has a name and presentation presumably intended to attract spacers on leave and others who simply find the idea of interplanetary travel and colonization romantic. Holos have turned much of the building's facade into what looks like a window into a black, starry void where astronauts and bioroids jet to and fro working to assemble the prefabricated segments of some vehicle, habitat, or other device.

This was promising, because I happened to know Los Scorpiones control the Far Frontier and thus might use it as a meeting site. It was also daunting, because while Nunez presumably wouldn't recognize me, gang members working security might, and if they decided I was tailing her even after Lívia had warned me away, they weren't likely to laugh it off and give me a second chance.

I pulled on my old flat cap, hurried back to a market stall I'd passed, and bought a No-Tells pill in the hope cap and pill together would further alter my appearance. The cap's bill would shadow my face, and the drug would make it go numb and slack. I'd still be able to talk with minimal effort, but I wouldn't have anything much in the way of facial expressions. Lots of poker players use similar methods to keep their opponents from reading them, so they shouldn't make me stand out from the crowd.

The burly doorman costumed in an imitation old-timey spacesuit complete with helmet passed me in without seeming to recognize me. Inside, the interplanetary motif continued. Additional holos veiled the ceilings in fresh views of space, and the handful of beeping, buzzing, chiming slot machines had pictures of rockets, comets, and stars on their spinning reels. The roulette wheels replaced the zero and double zero with stylized pictures of Luna and Mars.

These games and others notwithstanding, most of the space was devoted to poker just as you'd expect, and peering about, I saw that Nunez had sat down to play. I didn't recognize any of her opponents as members of Los Scorpiones, so it didn't appear the game was providing cover for a meeting. But maybe she'd arrived early and was killing time. In any case, having come this far, I wasn't inclined to leave off observing her. You never knew, I might learn *something*.

Unfortunately, she'd taken a seat in a high-stakes room where I couldn't follow unless I was able to participate in such a game. With a sigh, I converted the rest of Lívia's payoff into chips and felt like regular old impoverished me again.

I sat down at a table adjacent to Nunez's. Even with all my remaining bribe money in play, I still had a puny stack compared to everybody else in my game, and assuming that meant I was easy money, a couple of the other players visibly perked up at my arrival. I resolved to be a rock, fold every hand except near-certain winners, and so give myself maximum time to study Nunez.

She was playing Loony poker, named in honor of the first long-term mission to the Moon, during which, according to legend, the scientists discovered their sole deck of cards didn't have all fifty-two. Loony poker is a seven-card stud variant in which two cards are randomly eliminated from the pack, thus altering the probabilities—and the players don't know which cards are removed. Supposedly a savvy player can infer which cards are missing over the course of play and so gain an advantage over the rest of the table.

It soon became apparent that Nunez was no expert. She lacked patience and bluffed too frequently, sometimes when it should have been obvious someone was going to call. As her stack dwindled, she became even more reckless, as though sheer stubbornness would force the cards to fall her way.

I suspected I now knew why she was working with Los Scorpiones. Weyland paid her well, but not well enough to cover her gambling debts. Serving up victims for the gang's organ grinders was how she was settling up.

Having guessed that, I wondered if there was anything else to be gleaned at the moment, or if I should get up and leave before I lost the last of Lívia's money. I was still thinking it over when the gang boss herself appeared in a doorway and beckoned. Nunez got up from the table, and the two disappeared together.

I couldn't just charge after them instantly without giving myself away. I also couldn't delay very long lest I miss the entire conversation. I gave it another minute, then threw in my hand with a snarl, jammed my remaining chips back in the rack they'd come in, picked up my complimentary cerveza, and stood up. After that, I drifted around the room as though seeking a table where I imagined I'd have better luck. When nobody was paying attention, I slipped through the same doorway Lívia and Nunez had used.

I half expected to find an enforcer stationed on the other side and was all ready to explain I was only looking for the restroom. I didn't have to, though. No one else was in the hallway. Maybe Lívia's habit of traveling light, without bodyguards and other goons in tow, was working in my favor.

Other doorways led to private, luxuriously appointed poker rooms presumably reserved for true high rollers playing for *ultra-*high stakes. Only one door was closed, and I assumed Lívia and Nunez were palavering on the other side.

I went into the next room in line and shut the door behind me. No sound was coming through the wall. Even behind a closed door, I was reluctant to put the vidlenses back on and look like myself again, but I had to eavesdrop somehow. I blinked the command to turn the built-in directional mic up to full.

That worked. The sound was still a little muffled, but I could tell which voice was Lívia's and was confident a vocal recognition program could ID both beyond a reasonable doubt.

"Fitzgerald and Rincon should check into the Gran Hotel on the fifteenth," said the voice that must be Nunez's. "Hiraj should become available two weeks after that, and Villasenor and Okamoto early next month."

"Good," Lívia said. "I can move most of these organs the day we yank them out. But we need to discuss increasing the quantity."

Nunez hesitated a second, reluctant, I suspected, to object to anything the gang boss proposed. Then she said, "You know I have to be careful."

"Has anything happened to make you believe anyone's getting suspicious?"

"No." That made me feel an iota safer in that it suggested Yevtukh hadn't reported our interaction, nor had anyone else figured out Weyland HR had been infiltrated, not that it would matter if somebody caught me snooping here and now.

"And you're still gambling," Lívia said. "Still on that losing streak? Still playing on credit? You need to at least send us enough product to stay current on the vig. If I were you, I'd want to get out from under. Then we'll actually start paying you."

"It's just…it's murder," Nunez said.

"Isn't everything, really, one way or another? Just one big poker game where a few tough players win, and everyone one else busts?"

From her glum tone, Nunez didn't find that philosophical tidbit especially encouraging, but nonetheless, she said, "I'll try to send more. One or two a month, anyway."

"That's all I ask."

A couple more exchanges, and they exited the room. I stayed put and gave them time to get farther away.

I was still worried someone was going to catch me, but I was elated, too. With the audio I'd just recorded, the story was complete. I had the proof I needed to post it to my channel or peddle it to a bigger outlet. I just had to decide if I was willing to take the chance.

It might be stupid going on suicidal. Still, my rationalization that I'd just been discreetly satisfying my own curiosity was buckling. Having gotten this far, who wouldn't want to take the final step?

Still mulling it over, I put the vidlenses back inside my jacket and peeked out into the hallway. Nobody was there, so I ambled back into the room where I'd sat watching Nunez. She'd rejoined her game but, concentrating on the play, neither she nor anyone else at the tables paid me any attention.

I headed on into the front of the casino and toward a cashier machine to convert my remaining chips back into credits. Suddenly something gripped my forearm tightly enough to make me gasp.

I looked around. It was my old acquaintance Metal Arm from Hoyo Rojo and my involuntary visit to La Cocina who'd grabbed me with his prosthetic hand. Plainly, he recognized me despite my rudimentary disguise.

"Hi," I said. I tried to look calm and innocent, although with the No-Tells pill still numbing my face, I may have just looked like the dead man I was in imminent danger of becoming. "Is there a problem?"

"What are you doing here?" Metal Arm asked.

"Just trying my luck." I nodded toward the chip rack in my immobilized hand to sell the lie.

"What happened to your glasses?"

"I don't always wear them."

"Maybe not when you're snooping and don't want to be recognized. Let's go talk to Lívia."

This was bad. Metal Arm was no criminal mastermind, but he was smart enough to realize it was a hell of a coincidence if I just happened to wander into the Far Frontier at the same time Nunez and Lívia were meeting. The boss would think the same, and if she listened to what I'd just recorded, that would prove beyond a doubt that I'd been spying.

"What if I don't want to go?" I asked.

"You're going."

"Screw you." I poured what was left of my beer on his prosthetic.

Everyone has seen the trope in a thousand bad sensies. I've heard it dates all the way back to old-fashioned movies and TV. Get something electrical wet, and it shorts out in spectacular fashion.

But it doesn't work in real life. Most gadgets are made of sterner stuff. Certainly, cybernetic limbs, even the ones not covered in fake skin, are waterproof. Otherwise, those who have them wouldn't be able to shower.

I stared at the prosthetic as though amazed and aghast that nothing had happened. Metal Arm barked a laugh at my idiocy, and that's when I dropped the empty glass and drove the heel of my palm into his nose.

The sucker punch snapped his head back. Presumably it flooded his eyes with blinding tears and briefly stunned him, too. But the grip of the metal hand remained as tight as before.

In a moment, he was going to come back at me hard, and even if I'd been optimistic about beating a Los Scorpiones enforcer in something approximating a fair fight, that wasn't the situation here. Other gang members were going to rush to his aid. I grabbed him as best I as was able one-handed, pivoted, and tried a clumsy hip throw.

The move was either going to break his hold on me or apply incapacitating torque to my own arm. For a split second, a stab of pain made me fear it was the latter, but then, as he hit the floor, his fingers let go. I bolted for the exit and, as I dashed past the doorman, realized I'd dropped my chips in the scuffle. Oh, well; I wouldn't have been able to cash them in, anyway.

I hurried on, not knowing where I was ultimately going or how, just trying to put distance between the casino and me. As soon as it occurred to me, I tossed the cap in a trash can. I also peeled off my jacket and carried it under my arm. Changing my appearance again even slightly might improve my odds of survival.

I was actually hoping that being out in public among the crowds in Low Market would improve them more, that Los Scorpiones wouldn't want to hurt me in front of witnesses, but it was a stupid hope born of desperation, and really, I knew better. They were lords in these streets and could do whatever they wanted to a nobody like me.

I came to the edge of a plaza given over to the sale of used clothing. A few items retained some ability to glow or change color and did so dimly and sluggishly on the racks. A gang member, recognizable by the animated scorpion tattoo twitching on her hairless scalp, stood peering about on the opposite side of the circular space. I immediately started to turn away, but it was too late. She headed in my direction with her hand in her pocket, where it was surely holding a knife or some other close-up weapon. Bystanders alert enough to sense her intentions scurried out of her way.

I ran, and she pursued. I tried changing course to shake her off my tail and only succeeded in shortening my lead. After a couple minutes, a male gang member joined the pursuit. She'd probably called others, too, who were even now maneuvering to intercept me.

Sure enough, when I ran into a one-time traffic circle now serving as another open-air market, a Los Scorpiones enforcer in a long coat decorated with the gang symbol in red was waiting on the street that ran directly out the other side. My heart pounding, starting to feel winded, I veered left, and he followed. He was only a few yards behind me, and I suspected the pair who'd been chasing me for a few blocks weren't too much farther back.

An honest cop on patrol was unlikely going on impossible, but I cast about for anyone or anything that could help me. One of the vendors in front of me had skinny, scruffy-looking dogs, dwarf jaguars, and miniature bears in a pen. The holobanner overhead and the ballyhoo he was spewing via a throat mic proclaimed that these were the finest g-modded pets, superintelligent and perfectly behaved.

A different vendor was grilling sizzling scraps of beef and pork to make into sandwiches. Ignoring both his yelp of protest and the blistering heat, I snatched up two handfuls and sprang into the pen. My left foot snagged on the top of the low fence, and I almost fell, but not quite.

I ran in among the startled animals and flung the hot meat far and wide. Not so perfectly behaved after all, they lunged for it and, when two or more were after the same piece, fought over it. With luck, they'd serve as a makeshift barrier to slow my pursuers, maybe even snap at them if they imagined they were coming to wrest the food away.

I swung myself over the far side of the pen, dashed on between a grimy, battered permanent stall that looked like it had been there since Mercado Baja was established and what appeared to be a spanking-new smartcloth tent, and spied the mouth of an alley. Other alleys connected to it, and I made turns randomly until I finally had to stop and catch my breath.

As I panted, I listened for sounds of pursuit. All I heard was the normal constant background noise of Low Market, the drone of a million conversations, and snatches of music from countless clubs and bars. Maybe the immediate danger was over.

Maybe, but only an idiot would count on it. I kept my guard up as I skulked onward. Deciding to change my appearance yet again, I stopped along the way to put my jacket back on and, now reduced to tapping the meager funds in my old credstick again, buy a cheap straw toquilla hat of the kind worn mainly by tourists and some Montubios.

Before long, I spotted the entrance to a Metro station a block ahead. As far as I could see from a distance, nobody who looked like a Los Scorpiones enforcer was watching the people passing in the entrance. Hoping to catch the next tube-lev to anyplace that wasn't Low Market, I quickened my pace but kept on looking for a gang member ready to pounce.

I still didn't see one, and hope made me eager. I nearly forgot caution and ran the last few steps. I took a deep breath and made myself take a really good look around instead, not just at what was ahead of me but at what was behind.

Lívia was standing about where I'd been when I spotted the Metro station, and she'd plainly spotted me. Proving that her black leather duster truly did contain the rumored arsenal, she pulled a pistol from inside it.

I wasn't sure why she was getting it out right then. Dozens of people were wandering around between her and me. I dodged ahead of three more strolling side by side and then had full cover, or damn close. It seemed unlikely that even a coldblooded killer from Los Scorpiones would take a shot—or hit me if she did.

Yet my intuition, or maybe just my fear, screamed that I was in immediate danger. Heeding it, I darted through the gate and lunged onto the down escalator. The shot from the gun cracked into the wall behind me, and I realized it had been a self-propelled tracking round that veered around all those people in its way to find me. Fortunately, it just hadn't been able to manage that last right-angle turn.

But the next round would surely hit the target if Lívia fired from the top of the escalator while I was still stuck on it. I reared up, clambered onto the balustrade, and slid down it like it was a sliding board.

The metal surface was slippery and steep, and I shot off the end and slammed down on the floor, losing my new hat in the process. I scrambled up and ran on toward the digital signboard that indicated a westbound train was arriving on level two and the escalator that would take me to it.

About halfway there, I realized that if Lívia didn't catch me in the station, she might well guess I'd boarded the train and have enforcers waiting at the next stop. Though it kept me on level one for additional time when, for all I knew, Lívia would come off the bottom of the first escalator and spot me, I turned around and hurried toward an up escalator, a dauntingly distant one, instead.

I made it unattacked and rode the moving stairs back up to ground level. Lívia wasn't waiting at the top. Presumably she was now prowling through the crowds in the station.

Meanwhile, I was back in damn Mercado Baja, but if Los Scorpiones believed I'd hopped a train, maybe they'd stop hunting me in the immediate vicinity. Still wary, I tramped onward and eventually came to yet another Metro stop. As I rode the first escalator downward, I was no longer as scared of a bullet, laser, or monoblade piercing my insides in the next minute. It freed me up to worry about where I was going.

My apartment? No, Los Scorpiones might well be watching it.

A friend's place? Again, no. Even if I were willing to make my troubles theirs, the gang could have them under surveillance, too. Besides, I wasn't sure I *had* many friends. Mostly I had business associates, people I didn't trust not to sell me out if Los Scorpiones threatened them or offered a reward.

The police? I didn't trust them, either—definitely not to protect me over the long haul, not when they'd warned me not to chase this story in the first place.

A hotel of some sort? Maybe, but it needed to be so utterly downscale that it was reasonable to hope Los Scorpiones had never bothered to establish a connection there—that the place was paying a few creds in "taxes" to a low-level street gang if anyone was bothering to extort it at all.

Seeking such an establishment, I spent the next couple hours sneaking down to the darkest, filthiest depths of the undercity and bought a night's doss in a dormitory-like space where derelicts lay snoring on the cots and rat droppings littered the floor. It smelled like puke and garbage, too.

I found a spot and lay down with my vidlenses, credstick, and PAD stowed inside my coat and my arms wrapped around my torso, partly to further protect what passed for my valuables and partly in the hope my self-embrace would fend off the chill better than the thin, scratchy blanket.

Sleep didn't come easily. I was exhausted but also tense and wide-eyed with the aftereffects of danger barely survived. As I lay struggling to close my eyes and keep them closed, to *not* jump at every slight motion or soft sound I detected in the dark, it felt as if the night's events were the culmination of the fall begun years earlier. Recklessness had tossed me out of NBN, and now it had tumbled me all the way down to the bottom of the mountain.

CHAPTER 8

E ventually I gave up on being able to sleep, but at some point, I must have drifted off, because the next thing I knew, a stout, red-faced man was screaming, "Up and out! Up and out!" When people were slow to stir, he yanked their blankets away and kicked the undersides of their cots to jolt them.

It would be an exaggeration to say my fitful rest had cleared my head. But after I stumbled out into the gloom that passed for morning light this deep in the undercity, wolfed down tasteless lukewarm *humitas* from a vendor's cart, and found an out-of-the-way brick wall to lean against, I managed to consider my options. It didn't seem that I had many good ones.

I could make the story public and hope the results would put me beyond the vengeful reach of Los Scorpiones, but I didn't think that would happen. Perhaps what I had would bring the law down on them, and things would be difficult for a while: operations compromised, members lost to prison or police bullets. I couldn't imagine the cops would destroy the syndicate utterly, though, or that they'd watch over me for the rest of my life. Nor, now that disastrous reality had overtaken my dreams, did I have any hope that the story would cause such a sensation that NBN would want me back. No; eventually, retaliation would find me.

But I doubted surrender would serve me any better. I could hand over the evidence stored on my devices and beg Lívia for mercy, but I'd still be the guy who went snooping around after she paid him not to and learned things he wasn't supposed to know. On top of which, if I went to her in a posture of supplication, it would likely only rouse her contempt and make her doubt I could be trusted to keep Los Scorpiones' secrets over the long haul. Safer and more satisfying, then, to dispose of me. It would even serve as a warning to others.

The more I thought about it, the more it seemed my only real hope of survival was to flee New Angeles. My modest talent for disguise arguably hadn't served me all that well lately, but it ought to do better once I got out of Base de Cayambe.

Money was apt to be more of a problem. I could readily spend what little was left on the credstick, but accessing my charge accounts—they were pretty much all maxed out anyway—would leave a trail, and though Los Scorpiones weren't known for hacking, they could surely find someone who was to trace me.

Well, I might be able to make it out of town somehow: hitchhike, stow away on something, or walk if I had to. What then, though? Could I launch a new life in a new place with nothing at all to get me started, not even my own identity? Off-gridders have done it, but they generally began younger than I was, and I'd never envied them their way of life. And on top of that, despite my assignments overseas, New Angeles was the only real home I'd ever known. I didn't *want* to leave.

Underlying all this rumination, making every possibility seem even grimmer and more hopeless—if that was possible—was a strong dose of self-disgust. My deal with Lívia had given me safety, money, and even a new story to chase. It had solved all my problems. What an idiot I was to have thrown all that away and finished the process of wrecking my life.

I was pretty sure I hadn't done it merely for the reason Sugar had suggested: that I still identified with those who live on the plaza level. It wasn't even mainly because I was clinging to the fantasy that I could get my job with NBN back or another position almost as good.

As much as anything, I just wanted to be a real journalist again, someone whose work mattered and who didn't let anyone push him around. But believing my motives had been at least a little bit noble was little comfort when things had come to this. It was maddening that, against all the odds, I'd gotten the damn story, and yet it was powerless to save me.

Or was it? Smiling—more to convince myself I'd hit on a viable idea than because my fears had suddenly melted away—I headed for the mouth of what looked to be a quiet alleyway.

CHAPTER 9

I bought some gel and did my best to plaster my hair into the spiky look popularized by sensie star Ido Siegel. The goo added green and purple highlights as well. The look was too much for a man in his late thirties, but there were plenty of guys like me running around who clearly didn't realize that; so in theory, I now looked different without appearing clownishly conspicuous.

Stopping in a thrift shop, I bought somebody's old blue jacket that still smelled faintly of the cheap Pheromone-Plus! cologne he must have sprayed on in copious amounts. Thus disguised, I climbed back up from the lowest, most wretched level of the undercity to one where most people's lives are at least a little less desperate.

That makes them worth robbing, extorting, or peddling vice to, and thus I kept an eye out for members of Los Scorpiones. Mainly, though, I was looking for one of the street-corner stim dealers who report to Tony Wood.

I found one, a scrawny kid who looked about thirteen and, unexpectedly, Tony himself talking to the boy. He'd apparently needed to ask or tell him something. I hung back until Tony laughed, slapped the street dealer on the back, and sauntered on down the street. Then I followed.

I wasn't trying to sneak up on him exactly, just ease close enough to start a conversation. Alert and streetwise, he sensed me coming when I was still a few paces back and pivoted.

Tony was about my age, but thanks to g-modding, his features and slim body looked about eighteen. He could have pulled off Ido Siegel hair. He studied me for an instant and then said, "Zamora!"

"Hi, Tony."

"You're still in Base de Cayambe? Are you crazy?"

"Time will tell. I need a favor."

"You must be joking."

"It won't get you into trouble with Los Scorpiones. To the contrary. They'll appreciate it. I need you to pass them a message."

He didn't try to deny he talked to them. He knew I knew his stim came from the Lab. "What message?"

"Tell them I recorded audio of Lívia Teixeira and Elena Nunez's private conversation in the Far Frontier. Now I want a meeting, but it has to be with Lívia *and* Nunez."

"Who's Nunez? Never mind. Better question: Do you *want* to die?"

"Stop asking things like that. It's bad for my morale. Los Scorpiones can collect me at eight o'clock outside Owney's Bar." Owney's caters to ex-prisec and ex-military, which is to say, hard people who are mostly armed and might take exception to a disturbance. Also, Lívia sometimes drinks there, and there was a rumor that at one time, she and Owney were close. So I hoped Los Scorpiones wouldn't simply roll up and shoot me on the spot.

Tony smiled. "You know, I could kill you or turn you over to Los Scorpiones right now. That would make them *really* grateful."

With his mod-enhanced muscles, to say nothing of whatever weapon he was carrying, he could probably make good on the threat, but I wasn't worried. "Violence isn't your style except when it's absolutely necessary."

"True. Okay, I'll tell them."

With that settled, I cleared out of the area fast because I had little doubt that, in addition to relaying my message, Tony was also telling Los Scorpiones where I was right then. That meant I needed to be elsewhere.

I made it back down to the level where I'd spent the night without anybody intercepting me. I returned to my quiet alley and made my preparations for the meeting, then hid in a rundown sensie house playing old comedies starring nobody I ever heard of that weren't funny, or maybe I just wasn't in a laughing mood. It wasn't a great way to spend what might turn out to be the last day of my life, but I did get in a nap.

When it was time, I headed out to Owney's. At first, I made faster progress than expected, so I slowed down. It would be a bad idea to show up early.

I parked myself in front of the bar at eight exactly. A hopper that had been hovering high above floated down to the street, and Metal Arm got out, glowering. He'd sought attention for his broken nose. It was back to its original shape but still mottled with bruises.

"I hope that doesn't still hurt," I said. Maybe not a good idea to provoke him, but mouthing off was a way to try to trick myself into imagining I wasn't scared, and really, at this point, it wasn't likely to matter whether I was a smartass or not.

He cocked the metal fist back for a punch.

"Easy," I said. "You're taking me to meet with Lívia." I hoped. "She won't like it if I'm not in any shape to talk."

He grabbed me, spun me around, slammed me up against the side of the hopper, and patted me down. The search turned up my vidlenses, PAD, and credstick, all of which he transferred to his own pockets before shoving me into the hopper, where his partner, the other enforcer who'd picked me up before, was waiting.

I gave him a nod he didn't acknowledge, and the hopper flew up into the air, shifted sideways to avoid a slidewalk, and inserted itself into the flow of traffic. "Where are we headed?" I asked. Or tried. Despite my attempt to playact being a tough guy, my mouth had gone dry, and I had to swallow and try again before I got the words out.

Nobody answered.

"Is Elena Nunez there?"

"Shut up," Metal Arm replied.

I half expected my captors to fly me to some organ grinder's lair. It would have felt appropriate. But it eventually became apparent we were headed for the Base de Cayambe junkyard. Maybe nobody thought my insides were in good enough condition to command a decent price.

The junkyard dates back to the building of the Beanstalk and covers many square kilometers filled with hills of scrap metal, derelict hoppers, stray lengths of frayed buckyweave cable, and every other kind of discard you can imagine. Scavengers eke out a living salvaging what's still usable. Some even live in the middle of the dump in slums constructed out of trash. But once we flew over the wall and onward, our direction made it clear we were headed for a more secluded spot, where a person could conduct business unobserved and bury a body in garbage, to go undiscovered for years or even forever.

Sure enough, the hopper made its way to a spot well removed from any of the slums and floated down into a low space hidden among several towering mounds of trash. As soon as Metal Arm opened the door, the complex stink of rot and various sorts of chemicals wafted in. He grabbed me by the forearm and hauled me out into the open. His partner got out, too.

The waist-deep garbage drifts that covered other portions of the junkyard hadn't yet taken over there. You were still walking through used coffee cups and fast-food wrappers, but you didn't have to wade and flounder through.

Lívia and Nunez were waiting a few yards from where the hopper had set down. The former looked slightly annoyed and possibly just a shade regretful that things had come to this; the latter, disgusted at finding herself in such a filthy environment. The glare she gave me conveyed that she blamed me.

"Zamora," Lívia said. "You asked to meet. Start talking."

"Okay," I said, my pulse beating in my neck. "I imagine you want to know exactly what I know and how much I can prove. Your guy there has my PAD. Everything's on it. I can play it for you."

"Give it back to him," Lívia said.

Metal Arm did so with a scowl, like he suspected I'd hidden a gun or a bomb inside the PAD. I thanked him just to irritate him a little more, then, trying not to let my hands shake, pulled up the vid and turned the PAD so Lívia could watch easily.

The report wasn't up to my usual standards. Denied the use of the resources in my apartment, I'd stood the PAD on a crate in the alley to shoot new footage of myself and edited using the rudimentary controls in it and my vidlenses. Still, what with the shots of the corpses in the morgue and the incriminating audio from the Far Frontier, it was powerful stuff.

Clearly, Nunez thought so. She watched with growing horror, and when she heard herself on the audio recording, her mouth fell open as if I'd punched her in the stomach. A moment later, her face twisted into a snarl like she wanted to punch me back. Rounding on Lívia, she cried, "He can prove everything!"

"Calm down," Lívia said. "Let's see the rest of it."

There wasn't much more: just what was left of the audio and then me again, wrapping up.

"All right," Lívia said. "What have you done with this? Did you send it somewhere?"

"Kind of yes, kind of no," I replied, still straining to seem confident and unafraid. The report was the only card I had to play. If I acted like I believed it was an ace, maybe my captors would think so, too.

"Meaning what, exactly?" Lívia asked.

"I thought a lot about this situation," I said. "If I share what I know, you'll kill me in retaliation. If I don't, you'll still kill me to make sure I keep quiet—and just for being a pain in the ass. I only get leverage from the *possibility* the information will go out. So that's how it is. If you and I make a deal, you've got nothing to worry about. If we don't, then we all have a bad night together."

"I take it someone else has a copy of this and is supposed to release it if you disappear? Is there really somebody you trust to pick a fight with Los Scorpiones just to avenge your miserable life? Then I guess we'll have to find and kill them, too."

"You won't have to bother," I said. "I uploaded the file to a certain service. Not one I've ever used before; a different one you can't find in time. At ten, unless I've countermanded the instructions in the meantime, it's going to send what you just watched to NBN, other news agencies, the police, public posting sites, and last but not least, the Weyland Consortium.

"It's a funny thing," I continued. "Since I started poking around, people have told what an insignificant little person I am. But ultimately, that goes for all of us, doesn't it? I mean, it's all relative. To minimize bad publicity, Weyland will squash Nunez here like a bug. They and public outrage will force the police to come after Los Scorpiones even if they'd rather not. Rival syndicates will take advantage of your problems to move on your territory and operations. It's going to be inconvenient."

"Here's what you don't understand," Lívia said. "If we torture you, you'll do whatever you have to to make it stop."

"You might want to rethink that," I said. "What protections did I set up to control access to the file? Retinal scan? Then you'd better leave me my eyes. Facial recognition? Then you can't rearrange it too much. Fingerprint or signature? I'm going to need my hands. And obviously, if I die, pass out, or go into shock, I won't be in any shape to give you passwords or anything like that."

"It's not as much of a problem as you think." Lívia nodded to her underlings. "Get him ready."

Metal Arm and his partner moved in on me, and despite all the posturing I'd done so far, terror grabbed hold of me. I snapped a kick at the partner's knee even though I was sure it wasn't going to do me any good.

It didn't. He was expecting resistance and shifted out of the way. At the same instant, Metal Arm jabbed the rigid fingers of the cybernetic hand into my solar plexus.

It hurt and took away my ability to breathe. While I was struggling to inhale, the enforcers forced my arms behind me and crossed them. A restraint device slithered around my wrists and drew itself tight. Somebody slapped something between my shoulder blades, and it clung there. Metal Arm shoved me down on the nose of the hopper, and the other face of the plate on my back adhered to it. The gadget was a StickTite, and I wouldn't be getting off the hopper unless my captors let me.

Metal Arm tore open my shirt and pulled down my pants. Lívia reached inside her duster, brought out something that looked like a four-legged black metal tarantula, and set it atop my chest. Tiny curved hooks on the ends of its limbs slid into my skin as it started to crawl, the same way a cat will dig its claws in a little when it's walking around on top of you, not meaning to hurt you but just so its footing feels secure.

It stung, but, panting and sweating, I assumed there was far worse to come, and I was right. After wandering for a while, the tarantula stopped on the right side of my upper chest. A needle slid out of its underside into my flesh, and a flare of agony made me jerk. Apparently the spidery device was stimulating a nerve cluster.

More bursts of pain followed. Then the needle retracted, and the tarantula crawled onward, possibly because the nerves it had attacked were getting tired. After ten or fifteen seconds, it found another spot it liked, and the torture resumed.

I say resumed, but really, it didn't take long before anticipation and dread made the intervals when the spider was moving as excruciating as the times when the needle was in, albeit in a different way. I had to wonder where it would perch next, and how many more seconds I had before it did.

At first, I didn't want to give my captors the satisfaction to hearing me cry out. But it wasn't long before the pain slammed a first scream out of me, and after that I couldn't help myself and no longer cared anyway.

Finally—I'd lost all track of time and had no idea how long it had been—Lívia plucked the tarantula off me. "Had enough?" she asked.

God knew, I had. I wanted the torture to end so badly that nothing else mattered. But then, through the tears blurring my vision, I got a look at her expression and Nunez's, too. They were *sure* I was going to break, and that certainty that they could control me galled me as it had back in La Cocina.

"Tick tock," I croaked.

Lívia sighed and put the robot back on top of me. Shortly thereafter, it found its way to my crotch.

That was especially bad, and when Lívia lifted the tarantula off me again, I felt a surge of crazy gratitude. I wanted to thank her, please her, give her whatever it took to keep her from hurting me anymore. I drew on all that remained of my willpower to resist the impulse.

"Had enough?" she repeated.

"What time...is it?" I replied. "I bet we're running...out of time."

"Do you think that's a good thing? If the information goes out, there's no reason the torture shouldn't continue all that night. No reason not to cut you up and kill you."

"But you don't want it to go out."

"You're wasting time!" Nunez said. "Put the robot back on him!"

"Quiet," Lívia told her without looking back around. "All right, Zamora, I guess you're more stubborn than I gave you credit for. You stop the transmission, and I'll let you go."

"That's a good start," I said, "but it's not the whole deal."

She snorted. "You want to shake me down for money?"

"No. I want the pipeline into the Weyland companies shut down. I don't want any more people fired and sent down to the Gran Hotel so Los Scorpiones can scoop them up and kill them."

"Didn't we talk about this? You can't change the world."

"I don't have to live in the whole wide world. I do have to live in my little piece of it and in my own head. And if that doesn't make sense to you, let me put it this way. I need to win one. I need some damn respect."

"Fine," Lívia said. "We'll close down the operation."

"I wish I could take that at face value," I said. "But you have someone you answer to, someone who might not sign off on your decision. Kill Nunez. Without her, there can't *be* a pipeline, and if your offer is sincere, you have no further use for her anyway."

Lívia grimaced. "Damn you, Zamora. We *had* a deal. Everybody was going to win. Everything was going to be easy."

"Sorry," I said.

I still couldn't tell which way Lívia was going to jump. Nunez presumably couldn't, either, but she didn't like it that the gang boss hadn't simply rejected my demand out of hand. "This is ridiculous!" she snarled. "Put the robot back on him! We're running out of—"

So fast I could barely follow the motions, Lívia whirled, reached into her duster, brought out a pistol, and shot Nunez in the middle of the forehead. She may have been dead before she truly even realized it was coming.

"I never liked her," Lívia said. "Too whiny." She looked at Metal Arm. "Let him up."

Scowling at the way things were going, Metal Arm said, "Cuffs and StickTite, release," and then there was nothing holding me down except post-torture shakiness and weakness. That was almost good enough, but I managed to flounder to my feet and pull my pants up.

"Give me back my glasses," I said. "You can watch what I'm doing on the PAD."

The vidlenses told me it was ten to ten. Amazed I'd held out that long, I gave the combination of blink and murmured commands that got me to the proper Shadow Net site. Called TimeBomb, in case you ever need it.

"So," Lívia said, "you didn't set up retinal scans, facial recognition, or anything like that."

"It doesn't matter now, does it?"

I shut off the countdown I'd started, erased the file and my vidlenses, and looked around to make sure Lívia was satisfied. She was pointing the gun at me.

"Really?" I asked, and at that point, I no longer had to fake being unafraid, or at least, not too much. I felt more tired than anything else. Maybe the events of the night had wrung the emotion out of me, or maybe, after the robot spider, a bullet didn't seem so bad.

"You broke your word," she said. "Why shouldn't I break mine?"

"With Nunez dead, the pipeline's defunct regardless, and it can't have been *that* big a piece of Los Scorpiones' total revenue. Shooting me at this point seems sort of petty."

"To me, it seems like it would be sort of satisfying."

"Look at this way. You have a reputation for keeping your promises."

"Who will know if I don't?"

I nodded toward Metal Arm and his partner. "They will, and your reputation matters *inside* the gang as well as outside, right?"

She studied me for several more seconds, the gun never wavering. Then she returned it to an inside pocket of her coat. "Don't ever cross me again," she said.

"I'm not planning on it."

Lívia looked at her two underlings. "Bury her."

The interment only took a moment, because Metal Arm and his friend simply stuffed Nunez's corpse into the base of a hill of trash. Shaken loose, garbage tumbled down from up above to hide any trace of it. Then Lívia tossed the PAD back to me, and still trembling, I fumbled the catch and nearly dropped it. I was pretty sure I wasn't getting the credstick back, and Metal Arm didn't offer it.

"So," I asked, "can I catch a ride out of here?"

Lívia laughed. "Don't push it." She and the enforcers piled back into the hopper. The vehicle flew up into the sky and left me alone with the heaps of garbage, the various stinks, the moonlight, and the dim shadow of the Beanstalk, its edge splitting the junkyard into dark and darker.

CHAPTER 10

I called a couple cab services, but no one would pick me up in the depths of the dump. When I felt sufficiently recovered from my ordeal, I tottered in the general direction of the wall with dots of blood from the tarantula's claws and needle staining my shirt and pants from the inside. Soon I was lost in the maze of pathways twisting among the mountains of garbage.

I might have collapsed if I hadn't happened upon a couple scavengers. Somewhat to my surprise, they didn't rob me, murder me, or leave me to die. They took me to their shack, offered me leftover roasted "guinea pig" that I suspected was actually rat, and gave me moonshine, painkillers, and a pallet to sleep on. When I woke after noon the next day, they showed me the way out of the dump.

And that's the story, really. Obviously, I never posted it for the world at large to watch or crossed Los Scorpiones again in some other way. I'm still alive, right? I ended up like I started.

Well, worse off, actually. I had some new puckery little scars and, far more seriously, was a couple hundred creds closer to utter destitution. But then a funny thing happened.

I changed my reports, like you do sometimes change things up when you're desperate and have nothing to lose.

Mind you, I didn't change them all that much. They were still mostly the kind of sensationalism my audience likes. But I dialed back the sleaze a little and sprinkled in a bit of content that might actually do somebody some good. If I was on my way out anyway, I might as well finish on my own terms.

And my ratings and revenue came back up.

I doubt the upswing is because people care more about others than I gave them credit for. More likely, it's just the newness factor, the cheap thrill of easy moral outrage, or simply random fluctuation. But hey, maybe, and whatever the reason is, I'll take it.

ABOUT THE AUTHOR

Richard Lee Byers is the author of over forty fantasy and horror books including The Things That Crawl, The Hep Cats of Ulthar, This Sword for Hire, Blind God's Bluff, Black Dogs, Black Crowns, Ire of the Void, and the books in the "Impostor" series. He is perhaps best known for his Forgotten Realms novels. One of them, The Spectral Blaze, won Diehard GameFAN's award for the Best Game-Based Novel of 2011.

Richard has also published dozens of short stories, scripted a graphic novel (The Fate of All Fools), and contributed content to tabletop and electronic games.

Richard lives in the Tampa Bay area and is a frequent guest at Gen Con, Dragon Con, and Florida SF conventions. He invites everyone to follow him on Twitter @rleebyers, friend him on Facebook, and add him to their Circles on Google+.

IT IS THE FUTURE. THE WORLD CHANGED. PEOPLE DID NOT.

Humanity has spread itself across the solar system with varying degrees of success. The Moon and Mars are colonized. A plan to terraform the Red Planet is well underway, hindered only by a civil war that has broken out and locked down many of its habitation domes. On Earth, a massive space elevator has been built near the equator in the sprawling megapolis of New Angeles, stretching up into orbit. Known colloquially as "the Beanstalk," it is the hub of trade between the worlds, especially for the helium-3 that powers fusion reactors and the modern economy.

Discoveries in computing and neurobiology now allow a human mind to be stored electronically in braintapes and then emulated to create strong artificial intelligence. The same research also has given rise to sophisticated brain-machine interfaces that allow users to feed data into their neurons and experience the Network in a whole new way. Advances in genetics and cybernetics allow people to modify or augment themselves at will, pushing the boundaries of what it means to be human.

Enormous megacorporations, called "corps" by most, influence every facet of daily life: food, threedee, music, career choices. Jinteki and Haas-Bioroid redefine life itself, making clones and bioroids with artificial brains using the latest neural conditioning and neural channeling techniques. The Weyland Consortium owns a piece of everything that goes up or down the Beanstalk—and everything goes up or down the Beanstalk. And NBN shapes what the masses think and dream, with the most extensive media network ever conceived on Earth under its control.

Despite the technological advances, human nature remains as complex and dark as ever. The human and android officers of the New Angeles Police Department struggle to keep order in the largest city in human history, while hundreds of murders are committed every day. Human First, a violent anti-android hate group, stages protests and uses heavy sledgehammers to destroy the "golems," the androids it blames for all society's ills. Crime is rampant, with orgcrime outfits deeply penetrated into law enforcement, politics, and the megacorps. High-tech Netcriminals called "runners" use the Network to enrich themselves, oppose corporate hegemony, and experiment with new technology.

LOS SCORPIONES

As the twenty-first century progressed, the South American cartels lost ground to rival orgcrime syndicates. Their salvation came in the form of a visionary and ruthless leader named Mateo Cortes. Exterminating all who resisted, Mateo seized control of his own organization, Los Scorpiones. Foreseeing what New Angeles would become when the Weyland Consortium chose it for its world headquarters, he focused the gang's resources into entrenching itself there. As the Space Elevator Project built new towns out of nothing, Los Scorpiones was there to exploit and intimidate the migrant workers. As New Angeles grew around Weyland's efforts, Los Scorpiones grew with it. Mateo expanded his cartel through recruitment and by making a simple offer to rival cartels in the area: they could unite under his authority, or he would wipe them out.

The cartel's bloody origins and penchant for violence is manifest in Los Scorpiones' extensive involvement in crimes like gunrunning, murder for hire, extortion, human trafficking, and organ grinding. Even the more vicious and ambitious bosses of other orgcrime syndicates tend to treat Los Scorpiones with a certain circumspection. The cost of a feud is inevitably high even if the rival organization holds its own. Thus, today, the greatest threat to Los Scorpiones comes from internal conflict.

MATEO CORTES

Mateo Cortes and his twin brother, Gonzalo, were born into a prosperous, respectable family. Their father worked as a deputy to Ecuador's minister of agriculture. Their mother was the chief administrator of Hospital Alcívar in Guayaquil.

Everyone expected the twins would follow in their parents' footsteps, but from an early age, their wild streaks lured them into trouble. They skipped school often and, by high school, were experimenting with alcohol, marijuana, cocaine, stim, gambling, and more. Their parents, aghast at their delinquent activities, cut off the boys' funds and made every effort to deter them, but unsuccessfully. To pay for their vices, the boys worked as couriers for Los Scorpiones, who found that the boys' youth and clean-cut looks helped them avoid police attention. In due course, Mateo and Gonzalo were entrusted with bigger jobs and ultimately initiated into the gang.

It wasn't a promising time for two young men to cast their lots with Los Scorpiones. Rival criminal syndicates had squeezed the cartels in recent years and taken over valuable territory and operations. Violetta Ochoa, leader of Los Scorpiones, was pushing back but to no avail. As Mateo rose through the ranks, he saw a better way. Instead of fighting and losing costly wars in Guayaquil and Quito, Los Scorpiones should devote their energies to establishing themselves as the first orgcrime syndicate operating in the growing

New Angeles. They could so deeply embed themselves in the structure of the megapolis that nothing would ever dislodge them. Violetta, however, was unreceptive to these ideas.

When a major stim sting landed both brothers in prison, they connected with other, like-minded Scorpiones. Sold on Mateo's vision for the future, they formed a conspiracy to murder Violetta. By the time Mateo, Gonzalo, and their fellow conspirators were released, their coup was ready to commence.

By chance, Mateo overheard Gonzalo making a clandestine call to Violetta—he intended to betray the would-be killers in exchange for a place at her side. No sooner had the call ended than Mateo mercilessly strangled his twin brother. In the coming days, Mateo impersonated his dead twin and waited for an opportunity. Catching Violetta off guard, Mateo stabbed her to death with a monoblade. No one challenged his assumption of leadership.

Los Scorpiones has prospered under Mateo Cortes' leadership ever since. As Los Scorpiones grew and thrived in New Angeles, Cortes invited other cartels present in the burgeoning city to unite under his authority. Those who refused faced all-out war and soon submitted.

Today, Mateo's appearance as a gaunt, silver-haired old man belies his strength and brutality. His aristocratic air is heightened by the antique gold-headed cane he affects—though state-of-the-art medical treatments have kept him healthy and vigorous. The blade concealed inside the walking stick has yet to see use, but Mateo knows better than anyone that complacency is death.

Mateo's goals remain what they've always been: to advance the fortunes of Los Scorpiones and to safeguard his own position as head of the cartel. He treats his lieutenants with a cordiality that suggests he trusts them in both regards—but the truth is quite the opposite. Perhaps unsurprisingly, considering the circumstances of his own rise to power, Mateo suspects most, if not all, of his subordinates harbor ambitions to replace him. At any given moment, one might be

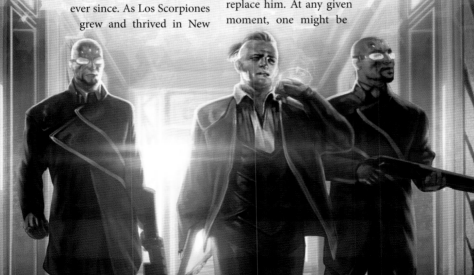

scheming to weaken another's position in a way that will adversely affect the syndicate as a whole. Even more seriously, one might be plotting to murder Mateo himself.

It is precisely because he cannot afford to trust anyone that Mateo hesitates to use his own people to investigate or thwart his lieutenants' schemes. Fortunately, New Angeles has prisec, mercs, and private detectives he can hire on the sly if need be.

VICTOR CORTES

Victor Cortes has lived his entire life in a world where his father is the unquestioned leader of the most successful drug cartel in Ecuador's history. While Mateo was born into a comfortable life, Victor was born into an opulent one.

Victor was no more interested than his father had been in school but felt no need to venture into sordid places and engage in dangerous activities to sample the world's pleasures. He took it for granted that they were already available to a boy as wealthy as him.

But Mateo didn't want his beloved son to grow up pampered and soft. He wanted him to become strong and crafty like his father, able to assume a leadership role in Los Scorpiones when the time came. Mateo required Victor to start where he did working for the syndicate—at the lowest level, doing jobs that were sometimes menial and often dangerous.

Mateo's plan worked. Though Victor barely escaped death on more than one occasion and served a prison term for arms dealing, he did rise through the ranks and grow into a fit leader for Los Scorpiones. Of late, though, Mateo wonders if his plan to forge Victor in his own image worked too well. Does Victor resent his father's harsh treatment? Has he become every bit as ruthless and ambitious as the man who strangled his own twin to secure power? After years of watching for murderous ambition among his people, has Mateo laid the groundwork for his own downfall?

Still, until Mateo decides his son is a liability, Victor remains the heir apparent, controlling a large number of gang operations. Most lieutenants have their favorites, and in Victor's case, it's a special enthusiasm for murder-for-hire and extortion. Indeed, he often participates in these activities personally.

Generally surrounded by bodyguards and hangers-on, Victor is a handsome man who looks much like

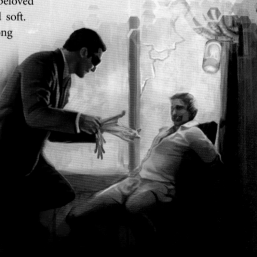

his father did at his age—or he would, if it weren't for the cosmetic surgeries and g-mods. In contrast to Mateo, who has opted for elegant but conservative attire in recent years, Victor prefers the latest, most flamboyant fashions New Angeles has to offer.

MIGUEL "MONSIGNOR" MORENO

It's an irony of organized crime that many members are also devoutly religious. Catholics, in particular, are well-acquainted with needing forgiveness for sin, and few sinners are more egregious than gangsters. For many years, Mateo Cortes has been a frequent congregant at the church of Father Miguel Moreno.

Moreno, once he became aware that the boss of Los Scorpiones sat in his pew, made extra effort to preach against the evils of orgcrime: drugs, murder, human trafficking—all the sins that Los Scorpiones so expertly commits. In private meetings with Mateo, he urged the mobster to turn away from his path, to no avail.

In one of these meetings, Moreno let slip that his church was in financial difficulty. The next collection day, he found over one million credits deposited anonymously into the church's account. Later, Moreno complained of disrespectful youth vandalizing the historic facade of his building. Three days later, the youths apologized and helped restore the damage. In hundreds of small ways, it seemed, Cortes and Los Scorpiones had become guardian angels of Moreno's parish.

The first time Moreno did a favor for Los Scorpiones in return, it was so simple and easy. He knew that the young man accused of murdering a rival drug pusher was a good child, simply misguided. So he lied to provide an alibi. The police eagerly accepted the word of such a respected community leader, and the young man in question became a devout member of Moreno's congregation—and continued to climb the ranks in Los Scorpiones. In time, Moreno's favors for the gang became more significant, and the gang's gifts more lavish. Soon, he developed a taste for the vices Los Scorpiones had to offer, and without knowing when he had passed the point of no return, he became a member of the gang in all ways that mattered.

Father Moreno maintains his position as a priest—for who would dare initiate proceedings to defrock him? A big, barrel-chested man with a rubbery face and a hearty manner, he dresses the part and is quick with a prayer, blessing, or verse to fit any occasion.

Today, Moreno carries on the sort of activities that brought him into the gang on a grander scale, as something of a PR rep for Los Scorpiones. He's a soft touch for anyone needing a handout and organizes block parties and fundraisers for the community. Only his fellow Scorpiones understand how Moreno uses the appearance of compassion to ease people into actions and attitudes preferable for the syndicate. He has an exceptional talent for luring people into Los Scorpiones' various illicit activities.

JUANA DELEON

Juana is a rarity among Los Scorpiones: a world-class pharmacologist with formidable academic credentials. Following a disastrous experiment in which she administered a "consciousness-expanding" drug of her invention to human subjects without approval from the oversight committee, she abandoned universities and legitimate pharmaceutical companies with their tiresome ethical standards and practices for the more freewheeling and lucrative word of the drug trade.

A petite woman with a wide, manic smile, Juana heads up "the lab," the gang's huge underground drug factory beneath Mercado Baja, where she concocts new drugs with boundless enthusiasm, sometimes experimenting on vagrants and on the gang's prisoners. Test subjects even include members of Los Scorpiones, as an act of penance for some slight or failure.

Deleon isn't solely in it for the science. Since the drug trade is the gang's biggest revenue source and she considers herself responsible for the never-ending flow of profits, Juana reasons that she deserves to succeed Mateo, and preferably sooner than later.

One might not think an academic like Juana could stand up to rivals who've lived a savage criminal life. But rumor, possibly spread by herself, has it that gang members ostensibly loyal to other bosses are addicted to a designer drug only she can supply. The other lieutenants fear that if they move against her, they'll find out the hard way where loyalties really lie.

ANTONELLA PUGA

When Antonella was six, she and her mother, Rebeca, were caught in a gunfight on the street, where a stray shot from a police officer's pistol hit Rebeca. Antonella watched her mother bleed out on the ground with no one coming to her aid. Afterward, she passed through a series of neglectful and abusive foster homes.

When she was eleven, Antonella fell in with a street gang with revolutionary pretensions. They claimed they were working to smash a corrupt and oppressive social order, and that sounded wonderful. If there was anyone who knew firsthand how unfair and uncaring the system could be, it was Antonella Puga.

In time, it became clear that the gang's talk of revolution was just that: talk. They were concerned only with money, pleasure, and respect from their peers, just like any common street gang. Still, having friends to watch one's back was better than being alone, and having creds, new clothes, and other amenities was preferable to the alternative.

After the arrest of key members broke up the gang, Antonella joined Los Scorpiones. By dint of cunning and courage, she rose through the ranks, her political notions seemingly abandoned.

Now that she's one of Mateo's lieutenants, though, Antonella has been distancing herself from the gang's day-to-day operations to focus on the activities of her alter ego, El Jefe. As the shadowy leader of the radical early reversion activist group La Brigada

Tricolor, she foments terrorism to destabilize the existing government of New Angeles. La Brigada's outrages include the murders of government officials and private citizens alike and the bombings of the NAPD headquarters building and the Root. The group also incited the riot that resulted in the burning of the undercity levels of the Haas-Bioroid Miloflores Arcology.

Antonella reassures her fellow bosses the goal is only increased power for Los Scorpiones. Some, however, view her as an overreaching fool likely to bring the wrath of the government down on their heads. They hesitate to move against her, though, because of the fanatics she commands entirely apart from the gang. Who knows how many of those La Brigada zealots there are or how much damage they could do if turned against Los Scorpiones?

The tall, charismatic woman either zealously endorses the goals of La Brigada or claims to be cynically exploiting the true believers, depending on who's listening. Her true feelings are an open question, one that even she may be unable to answer.

LÍVIA TEIXEIRA

Lívia grew up on the streets in the most wretched, desperate poverty Base de Cayambe can provide. The military offered an escape, and using a stolen identity to conceal her age and extensive juvenile arrest record, she enlisted.

She thrived in the army until she got into an altercation and accidentally killed an officer. Recognizing that a court martial was unlikely to go well for her, she fled, once again changed her identity, and joined Los Scorpiones, where her combat training and keen intuition helped her rise to become a boss. As she prospered, cosmetic surgery and g-modding kept her up with ever-shifting trends as ably as any sensie star. Perhaps, too, it was one way of distancing herself from the lives she'd left behind.

Unlike most of the upper ranks of Los Scorpiones, Teixeira doesn't make the other bosses feel particularly paranoid. She doesn't appear to aspire to take Mateo's throne. She doesn't seem to be amassing a powerbase of underlings loyal first and foremost to her. Operating as a sort of troubleshooter at large, she often serves as a peacemaker among factions when there are disputes and as a formidable enforcer when somebody's operation runs into trouble from outsiders, a service she provides for a cut of the proceeds.

Notably, Lívia takes a special interest in bringing new members into the fold. It's not impossible these recruits retain some loyalty to her even if they end up paying nominal allegiance to another boss. Being on good terms with the other lieutenants helps her learn the details of their operations, including, perhaps, their vulnerabilities. If Lívia did have her sights on Mateo's crown, the other bosses would have plenty of reason to worry.

LA COCINA

Los Scorpiones controls any number of stim dens, brothels, safe houses, and similarly illicit or fringe locations throughout Base de Cayambe. They operate a huge underground factory for recreational drugs, referred to simply as "the Pharmacy." But they often conduct strategy sessions, other internal meetings, and the friendlier sort of discussions with outsiders at La Cocina, a dining establishment that's thrived under their patronage (and made the *Cayambe Chronicle*'s list of best-kept culinary secrets five years running).

Even certain criminals who aren't cartel members have gotten into the habit of meeting at La Cocina to talk business. While Los Scorpiones reliably keeps the place clear of any police presence, there are no guarantees against eavesdroppers—or bugs placed by their courteous hosts.

La Cocina is based in a centuries-old, five-story brick building with red terracotta shingles. The interior features traditional Mission decor with bright colors, wrought-iron railings, potted flowers and trees, fountains, and waterfalls, the effect enhanced by outdoor vistas displayed via holograms and vidscreens. Everything combines to create a nostalgic vision of old Ecuador, of an era whose real-life vestiges New Angeles has mostly swept away.

The public part of the restaurant occupies the first three floors, where low-level members of Los Scorpiones sometimes talk day-to-day business. High-level discussions take place in private rooms on the top two floors.

On first inspection, La Cocina looks like a soft target. A rival syndicate might think that a well-timed raid could decimate Los Scorpiones and eliminate its leaders. But rumor says the building contains secret fortified rooms stocked with weapons and a number of concealed escape routes.

Patrons of La Cocina soon come to recognize a number of the people who work there. Valentino Sastre, the owner, is a plump man with a black handlebar mustache. He often circulates through the dining rooms chatting with customers and making sure their meals are to their liking. He is every bit the jovial restaurateur or tavern keeper seen in sensies, an image he cultivates to reinforce the restaurant's ambiance.

Valentino also works hard to avoid knowing any more than necessary about Los Scorpiones business and orders his staff to do the same. It is, he tells them, to everyone's benefit.

Most take the warning to heart, but Magdalena Felix, a quiet young busser, doesn't—at least, not always. Magdalena's father was found guilty of manslaughter following an altercation with his girlfriend's abusive ex-husband. In the year since he was put away, Magdalena has become desperate for creds. A lawyer claims he can get the conviction overturned on appeal, but his services don't come free. As it turns out, the information Magdalena sometimes overhears can be valuable to the right people. She's gotten away with it so far.

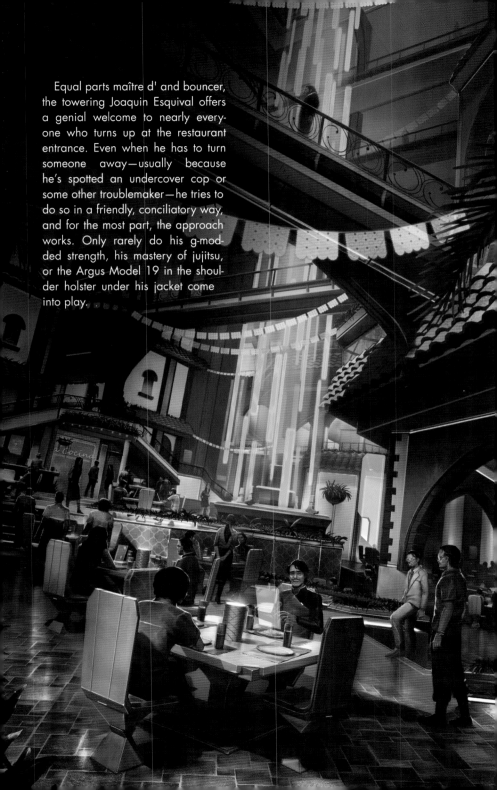

Equal parts maître d' and bouncer, the towering Joaquin Esquival offers a genial welcome to nearly everyone who turns up at the restaurant entrance. Even when he has to turn someone away—usually because he's spotted an undercover cop or some other troublemaker—he tries to do so in a friendly, conciliatory way, and for the most part, the approach works. Only rarely do his g-modded strength, his mastery of jujitsu, or the Argus Model 19 in the shoulder holster under his jacket come into play.

RELATIONSHIPS WITH OTHER CRIMINAL ORGANIZATIONS

Los Scorpiones regard all of New Angeles as theirs, but the reality is that it's impossible to keep other orgcrime out of the city or even Base de Cayambe. Still, no one profits from endless war, and Mateo and his lieutenants generally seek to get along with the rest of the underworld, although it's not unknown for a dispute to explode into violence.

THE MAFIA

Los Scorpiones and the Mafia maintain an amiable and cooperative relationship, in part because the two organizations are careful not to directly compete. Los Scorpiones are apt to call on the Mafia for help with money laundering and fencing stolen merchandise. The Mafia sometimes deems it safer or expedient to hire Los Scorpiones muscle or contract killers than deploy its own.

Mutual usefulness doesn't always mean mutual respect. There are those among Los Scorpiones who see the Mafiosi as relics who've gotten old and soft, while some Mafiosi regard Los Scorpiones as wild, undisciplined punks. Such attitudes rarely poison negotiations, and it seems unlikely the cooperation between the two groups will break down anytime soon.

14K

Los Scorpiones has a fierce rivalry with the triad called 14K. The two groups compete in the drug and weapon trades, and while the competition has always produced a certain amount of friction, the situation has deteriorated nearly to the point of war. Each has accused the other of encroaching into their turf in Mercado Baja, where La Calle de los Gorriones is the traditional boundary.

In reality, neither group is to blame. In her guise as El Jefe, Antonella Puga has had members of La Brigada Tricolor impersonate members of both gangs and foment trouble. By doing so, she hopes to draw Victor into a deadly and fruitless conflict to weaken his position.

Lívia Teixeira has taken an interest in the situation. Given that she appears to be on equally good terms with Victor and Antonella, it's uncertain what use she will make of the truth if she finds it.

THE YAKUZA

Historically, Los Scorpiones have had little interaction with the Yakuza. The latter mainly operates out of Nihongai, where Los Scorpiones has little presence. The two groups rarely compete in the same activities, and the closed, ultrasecret nature of the Japanese syndicate prevents meaningful collaboration.

Recently, though, runners employed by Mateo have stumbled across evidence of Yakuza runners raiding Los Scorpiones data, presumably for any information they can turn to their profit. Mateo is currently pondering what, if anything, to do about it.

If he does retaliate, it won't be in cyberspace. His runners are good, but not as good as Yakuza Netcriminals. Retribution will come in the form of a bloody strike.

ENTERPRISES

Los Scorpiones currently derive their largest revenue from the drug trade. Beyond this, however, the gang is notorious for crimes involving violence—or at least the threat of it.

MURDER FOR HIRE

Los Scorpiones boast that they can kill any target. They often do it fast, with a minimum of risk and fuss. But if the customer wants it and is willing to pay extra, they'll make an example of the victim, often by performing the deed in a very public place or simply dumping the horribly mutilated corpse where it's sure to be discovered.

When a public hit is required, the killer or kill team sometimes uses gas bombs specially prepared by Juana Deleon. The gas induces an ultraheightened fear state that renders bystanders helpless to interfere and ensures suitably terrified witnesses.

HUMAN TRAFFICKING

Once a pillar of Los Scorpiones operations, human trafficking has become almost obsolete with the rise of androids. Androids are completely obedient without drugs or conditioning, even more disposable, and generally less trouble—and they're getting cheaper every year. But so far, at least, there are still customers who prefer genuine human beings, and as long as that's the case, Los Scorpiones won't abandon a business they've learned to conduct with ruthless efficiency. In the meantime, kidnap for ransom is a profitable trade that uses much of the same infrastructure and skills.

New Angeles sees a constant flood of immigrants seeking a better life. Meanwhile, the undercity teems with the desperate poor. Thus, Los Scorpiones find plenty of vulnerable souls to draw into their keeping, some with blandishments and false promises, some by the simple expedient of snatching them off the street. However these people are obtained, Juana's drugs help keep them compliant when the gang sets them to work or sells them to other criminal syndicates, private citizens, or even supposedly reputable corporations operating off-the-book sweatshops.

ARMS TRAFFICKING

Successful arms trafficking requires connections with vendors, warehouses, and shipping companies. Superior arms trafficking requires contacts inside corporations like Argus and Skorpios, companies that manufacture state-of-the-art weapons. Fortunately for their customers, Los Scorpiones have these, thanks to a combination of payoffs and blackmail.

Once weapons are acquired, getting them to buyers is little more complicated than in centuries past. If the customer isn't in New Angeles, the Mafia puts its worldwide smuggling operation at Los Scorpiones' disposal in exchange for a share of the proceeds.

Shipping weapons to criminals, terrorists, and others who aren't supposed to have them on Luna and Mars is trickier, involving moving the contraband up the Beanstalk and then via freighter or cargo pod. Given the added expense, the delay, and the fact that both colony worlds now have their own manufacturing bases, only a relative few Loonies and Martians purchase Los Scorpiones' merchandise. Occasionally, though, someone wants a prototype weapon or some other item only available on Earth.

When that happens, the Mafia can smuggle items off-planet as well, but the supply chain isn't as evolved and secure as its network on Earth. Some members of Los Scorpiones, including, notably, Juana Deleon, worry about a snafu that could bring serious heat down on the gang.

ORGAN GRINDING

"Organ grinding," the forcible removal and resale of human body parts, both natural and implanted, is the crime for which Los Scorpiones are most infamous. Just as Base de Cayambe's countless poor and the endless influx of new arrivals provide abundant fodder for human trafficking, so too do they serve up easy marks for predators who subdue victims with drugs or violence and whisk them to hidden dissection rooms.

While corrupt or disgraced physicians may be involved, it's more often someone with less comprehensive or conventional medical training who takes the victims apart.

The surgeon may be after a particular organ or cybernetic to fulfill a customer's request, but they often just harvest anything that looks healthy and commands a good price on the black market. Essentially, it's not unlike breaking down a stolen hopper in a traditional chop shop.

Harvested body parts go to the clinic, legitimate or otherwise, that ordered them, or for sale on the Shadow Net. If the victim survives the surgery, most Scorpiones consider it safer and easier to finish them off. But occasionally a survivor escapes or, on a captor's whim, is simply released and subsequently found tottering through the undercity clutching their bloody scars.

Like human trafficking, organ grinding is a business in transition. Historically, it was based on the fact that stolen organs—both natural and artificial—were cheaper or more available than those obtained through legitimate channels. To some degree, that's still true, but advances in the production of both cloned and mechanical organs have cut into the profit margin on standard items.

Accordingly, Los Scorpiones have become increasingly interested in expensive, exotic implants like g-modded organs or the very finest cybernetics, improvements that enhance the body's functioning beyond natural limits. For these, demand and profit margin are still high. The problem is that potential victims who possess them—most often soldiers on leave and prosperous citizens slumming in the mean streets of the undercity—are more likely to draw heat than unknown immigrants and the poor. Nonetheless, Los Scorpiones are reluctant to pass up the money they represent and are working on ways to finesse the problem.

ANDROID

SHADOW OF THE BEANSTALK™

NEW CONTENT

The following pages present additional content for *Shadow of the Beanstalk*, a sourcebook for the *Genesys* Roleplaying Game that allows you to enter the worlds of *Android*.

To use this content, you will need a copy of the *Genesys* Core Rulebook and *Shadow of the Beanstalk*.

NEW ADVERSARIES

The following game profiles allow GMs to include Lívia Teixeira and Miguel Moreno in their *Genesys* games. Of all Los Scorpiones' bosses, these individuals are particularly likely to interact with PCs in a variety of ways, thanks to their particular roles within the syndicate. Both characters rarely go anywhere without gang *cascares* (see page 222 of *Shadow of the Beanstalk*) to serve as bodyguards and fulfill any other tasks the bosses request.

MIGUEL MORENO (NEMESIS)

"Monsignor" Moreno prefers to delegate the unsavory matters of Los Scorpiones business to his cascares, but is always ready to advocate for the gang. Although he often does so subtly, in the role of impartial priest and community pillar, he can be as threatening as any boss when the situation warrants.

BRAWN	AGILITY	INTELLECT	CUNNING	WILLPOWER	PRESENCE
2	2	3	3	2	4

SOAK VALUE	WOUND THRESHOLD	STRAIN THRESHOLD	M/R DEFENSE
4	14	18	0 | 0

Motivations: Desire (Wealth), Fear (Exposure), Strength (Charismatic), Flaw (Greed).

Skills: Charm 5, Cool 1, Deception 4, Leadership 3, Negotiation 4, Perception 1, Ranged (Light) 2, Streetwise 2, Vigilance 1.

Talents: Adversary 1 (upgrade difficulty of all combat checks against this target once), Laugh it Off (when targeted by a social skill check, may spend ♻ ♻ ♻ or ❂ to reduce any strain the check inflicts by 5. Then the character who targeted Moreno suffers strain equal to the amount of strain reduced).

Abilities: Fallen Figure of Faith (when making a social skill check to inflict strain, inflicts 2 additional strain, unless target knows Moreno's Fear or Flaw Motivations).

Equipment: Snub pistol (Ranged [Light]; Damage 6; Critical 3; Range [Short]; Inaccurate 1), priest's robes, rosary, silver case of Lo-Fi capsules, personal Bible with snub-pistol-shaped hollow space inside.

LÍVIA TEIXEIRA (NEMESIS)

As glamorous as she is deadly, Teixeira's duties as recruiter and gang boss bring her into contact with a variety of New Angeles' residents. For the fortunate ones, a meeting means potential business opportunities. For the less fortunate, it might be the last meeting they ever take. In either case, refusing Teixeira's invitation is rarely an option.

BRAWN	AGILITY	INTELLECT	CUNNING	WILLPOWER	PRESENCE
3	3	2	4	4	2

SOAK VALUE	WOUND THRESHOLD	STRAIN THRESHOLD	M/R DEFENSE	
4	18	14	0	0

Motivations: Desire (Power), Fear (Humiliation), Strength (Ruthlessness), Flaw (Cruelty).

Skills: Athletics 2, Brawl 4, Coercion 4, Cool 2, Discipline 4, Knowledge (Society) 3, Leadership 3, Perception 2, Ranged (Heavy) 4, Ranged (Light) 4, Resilience 2, Streetwise 5, Vigilance 2.

Talents: Adversary 3 (upgrade difficulty of all combat checks against this target three times), Deadeye (After inflicting a Critical Injury and rolling the result, may suffer 2 strain to select any Critical Injury of the same severity to apply to the target instead).

Abilities: Los Scorpiones Boss (may spend a maneuver to direct all Los Scorpiones characters in the current encounter; each may immediately perform a free maneuver or add ❂ to the results of their next check), Extreme G-modded Physique (before making an Athletics, Brawl, Melee, or Resilience check, may suffer 1 strain to add ❂ ❂ to the results).

Equipment: Skorpios Stalker V pistol (Ranged [Light]; Damage 4; Critical 2; Range [Medium]; Guided 2, Pierce 4, Vicious 2), Skorpios Stalker V rifle (Ranged [Heavy]; Damage 4; Critical 2;

Range [Extreme]; Guided 3, Pierce 4, Vicious 2), 4 monofilament grenades (Ranged [Light]; Damage 7; Critical 3; Range [Short]; Blast 7, Limited Ammo 1, Vicious 2), G-modded fists and feet (Brawl; Damage 5; Critical 3; Range [Engaged]; Disorient 1, Knockdown, Sunder), trenchcoat with hidden pockets and holsters (+1 soak), cocktail dress.

NEW WEAPONS AND GEAR

These items are particularly favored by some members of Los Scorpiones, and PCs can obtain them as normal.

STALKER V

The Stalker V, from Skorpios, is in most ways a conventional fletcher, but each 6mm steel dart has an onboard microprocessor that links back to the weapon's integrated sensor suite, along with adjustable vanes and a terminal-phase booster. They're as much a miniature missile as a flechette dart.

When fired, the weapon's sensors "flag" the intended target, then automatically guide the flechette around obstacles and debris, compensating for the target's movements all the while. When the flechette has a straight shot, it fires its explosive booster for an extra boost of penetrative power—often punching right through its target.

Skorpios has made a pistol and rifle variant of the Stalker, although so far the weapon has only seen limited sales due to its cost; either variant of the gun is extremely expensive, and the guided flechettes can only be purchased directly from Skorpios-licensed distributors.

RANGED WEAPONS

NAME	SKILL	DAM	CRIT	RANGE	ENCUM	HP	PRICE	RARITY	SPECIAL
Stalker (Pistol)	Ranged (Light)	4	2	Medium	2	0	1,450	9	Guided 2, Pierce 4, Vicious 2
Stalker (Rifle)	Ranged (Heavy)	4	2	Extreme	4	1	2,200 (R)	9	Guided 3, Pierce 4, Vicious 2

ENFORCED COMPLIANCE DEVICE

Known on the street as the "tortantula," the ECD is a truly horrifying little robot. Resembling nothing more than a palm-sized, four-legged spider covered in a shiny black metal carapace, the tortantula crawls all over its victims with its tiny, barbed feet. When the device senses the bioelectrical traces of a nerve cluster beneath it, it sinks a long, vicious needle into the flesh to overload the nerves with blasts of current.

As information gained from torture is both notoriously unreliable and inadmissible in court, ECDs find most use at the hands of orgcrime and certain corp departments that value the discreet visible scars the device leaves, which are easily overlooked or explained away.

While a character is subject to an ECD, all Coercion checks targeting them add ✹ ✹ ⟳ ⟳ and double the amount of strain they inflict.

NEXT STICKTITE

In its inert state, this high-tech personal restraint device looks like a flattened, grey jellyfish. When the device is applied to a person (usually on their back between the shoulder blades), the electro-reactive polymer "tentacles" wrap tightly around the subject's torso and arms. The device's flat plate can adhere to almost any surface, sprouting millions of polymer "hairs" that burrow into the microscopic imperfections found on any material.

Your character can apply a StickTite to an engaged character using a maneuver and activating it via a spoken command (generally the target should be staggered, immobilized, or at least prone before your character can use a StickTite on them). Once the StickTite activates, the target is immobilized. They can only escape by making a **Formidable (◆◆◆◆◆) Coordination check**. The StickTite can be deactivated via spoken command (as an incidental).

GEAR

ITEM	ENCUM	PRICE	RARITY
Enforced Compliance Device	1	1,000	8
StickTite	2	200	5